BOLO
The Annals of
the Dinochrome Brigade

BOLO

The Annals of
the Dinochrome Brigade

KEITH LAUMER

ARC MANOR
ROCKVILLE, MARYLAND

✱

SHAHID MAHMUD
PUBLISHER

www.CaezikSF.com

ISBN: 978-1-64710-034-6

First CAEZIK Notables Edition. First Printing. September 2021.
1 2 3 4 5 6 7 8 9 10

CA≡ZIK
NOTABLES
An imprint of Arc Manor LLC

www.CaezikSF.com

This book is dedicated,
with affection and respect,
to

Ben Bova

Contents

INTRODUCTION

INTRODUCTION
by Jack Campbell (John G. Hemry)

In the mid-to-late 1960s and early 1970s, Keith Laumer was one of Those Writers. The ones a lot of people couldn't wait to see new stories from. Whether he was taking you across the multiverse to *Worlds of the Imperium*, or making you laugh as Retief saved the day once again, or writing the purest space opera ever in works like *Galactic Odyssey*, Keith Laumer could be counted on for a great story. It's a measure of how well he told stories that when I went through those in this collection, I found I remembered nearly every detail of them, even though it's probably been at least thirty years since the last time I'd read them. I read one hell of a lot of books and stories in the 1960s and 1970s. But while many are only vague memories, I remember Laumer's.

And, then (in an almost mythic way) Keith Laumer became a living example of his greatest and most memorable literary creations. If you haven't heard of Keith Laumer before this, that's why.

But before that happened, he wrote a lot of great stories. Not the sort of stories that literary critics swoon over, but the sort of tales that took readers on wild rides and left them wanting more. That's partly due to plot, of course, but as with any good story it was also about the characters. As a rule, the beauty of Laumer's characters lay in their authenticity. You accepted them, because you knew those people. You'd worked with (or for) people just like them, grabbed a beer with people like them, argued with people like them. You'd dealt with bosses who were just as short-sighted and clueless as the bosses they had to deal with. And if they were a bit too capable and a bit too confident (such as Retief) they still came across as borderline believable and as someone you would like to spend time with.

This collection is about a certain subset of Laumer's stories, though. Stories about a line of armored fighting vehicles known collectively as Bolos. Stories which drew on his military experience to create weapons which were characters as believable as his humans. There's a famous cartoon from World War II (drawn by Bill Mauldin) that shows a jeep in a ditch with a broken axle. Next to the jeep is a veteran cavalryman, looking away, his face twisted in pain, the barrel of his .45 caliber pistol aimed at the hood of the jeep as he prepares to put his faithful mount out of its misery. That's how people in the military see the equipment they work with. A tank, an aircraft, a ship, isn't a thing. In its own way, it's alive. Every ship I sailed on had her own personality. Every time I heard that a ship I'd sailed on had been broken up, or sunk as a target, I felt like I'd lost a friend, or a least a co-worker.

But to the military as an institution, to the government, all of those ships and aircraft and tanks are just equipment. Use them, and when they're no longer useful, dispose of them. And that can carry over to the treatment of veterans, who might find themselves abruptly discharged when no longer needed, or fighting to get necessary medical treatment w7357hen dealing with service-related injuries. I believe the Bolo stories were at least in part pushback against that kind of official inhumane attitude toward those who'd served loyally and well, right up until they weren't needed any more. (One painful example of that bureaucratic approach is that until the year 2000, US military working dogs were officially classified as "equipment" that couldn't adjust to civilian life. When the military was done with them, the dogs were put down. When we pulled out of Vietnam, our military working dogs were left behind. They were only equipment, after all. Officially, not worth saving.) That's the atmosphere, the official attitude, that Keith Laumer personally experienced. I have no doubt that formed part of the motivation for some of the stories included here.

That military experience is an aspect of Laumer's life that you see reflected in other ways in his writing, especially the Bolo stories. It's something that's hard to explain to someone who's never served in the military, but I think the best word might be "belonging." I'm not talking about anything fancy like esprit de corps. No, I mean the sense that you're where you should be and doing what you should be doing because that's where part of you will always belong. I'm a sailor. I always will be. It's been decades since I rode a Navy ship to sea, but I still belong there. A lot of other vets feel the same. Part of them will always be a soldier or an airman. In the case of Marines, the idea is formalized. There are officially no "ex-Marines." Former Marines, yes, but once a Marine, always a Marine. You don't just remember the people you worked with, you remember being one of them.

Laumer clearly felt that. Something about the Air Force kept calling him back. He served in the US Army Air Force in the last part of World War II, later joined the Air Force from 1953-1956, spent some time in the US Foreign Service in Burma (you didn't think those Retief stories were built on pure imagination, did you?), then rejoined the Air Force from 1960-1965, departing as a captain. He left the Air Force, until he came back, then he left the Air Force, until he came back, only finally leaving it in 1965 to become a full-time writer. (Believe it or not, in the 1960s it was possible to earn a living wage just by writing short stories for magazines. Write some books? You could live pretty well on that.)

You can see this sense of belonging in Laumer's stories. Bolos define themselves as part of their unit. That's what they are. Thrown into an unfamiliar situation, they fall back on that. The soldiers who worked with them, their commanders, still feel the old bonds across decades of distance. Even when they're no longer needed, those old soldiers and their Bolos still need each other. Laumer let everyone feel that bond.

Aside from the human aspects of the stories, Laumer also had a genius when it came to naming weapons. Hellbore. Infinite Repeater. Crater Gun. Continental Siege Unit. (A friend of mine once wondered how you'd lay siege to a continent, and why anyone would want to. I think anime offers the answer to that, with its proud and frequent embrace of the idea that if something is cool it doesn't necessarily have to make sense.) Those names offered a veneer of technical reality to the science fiction. That's vital in any good SF. No matter how advanced the technology, it has to feel real.

For all that, Laumer didn't let reality hold him back. Despite the SF trappings, there was always an element of fantasy to the Bolo. The first Bolo (MK 1 Mod B) is described as massing 150 tons. That's not impossible. The largest "super heavy" tank ever built, at roughly 200 tons, was the German Maus (which means Mouse, because even those efficient, no-nonsense Germans have a sense of humor). Since the Maus was too heavy to use bridges, it was designed to cross rivers by buttoning up and rolling across the bottom. But the Bolos kept getting bigger, culminating in the MK XXXIII which was described as weighing 32,000 tons. That compares to a modern Arleigh Burke class destroyer displacing about 10,000 tons, and Iowa class battleships which displace 50,000 to 60,000 tons. A MK XXXIII Bolo probably didn't worry about steering around anything in its path, instead just going through or over any obstacle.

We're also still far from the Artificial Intelligences that increasingly controlled the Bolos and created the best stories about them. Well into the 21st Century, our most advanced software is no more self-aware than a slide rule. But it's the job of an SF writer to imagine things to come, and how we should deal with those things. Laumer's stories effectively make us think about *how* we should deal with the smartest of smart weapons before we *have* to deal with them.

Some things in Laumer's stories are dated. That's inevitable. SF does a particularly lousy job of anticipating social changes. But some things hold up very well. The end of The Last Command, with the Bolo plaintively asking how far it is to maintenance as its power fails, echoes the more recent meme of the Mars rover Opportunity transmitting "my battery is low and it's getting dark." Opportunity didn't actually send that (its last transmission was technical data that added up to the same thing) but the popularity of that meme speaks to the way all humans (not just veterans) think of our machines as living creatures.

Given all of that, why haven't you heard more of Keith Laumer? In 1971, at the top of his game, he had a severe stroke. It paralyzed half of his body, shredded his creative skills, and warped his personality. From 1971 until his death in 1993, Keith Laumer fought against that, constantly battling pain to try to physically recover, stubbornly continuing to write even though the magic was gone, and earning a reputation as a short-tempered, explosive jerk. His stories from that period hold none of the magic he'd once shared. Those who read only his later work didn't realize how good his earlier stories had been. Those alive today who remember Keith Laumer from personal meetings are overwhelmingly those who remember him after the stroke. And that Keith Laumer was a difficult man.

Hence the mythic fate of a once-great writer. In the end, Keith Laumer came to resemble one of his abandoned Bolos. Battle-scarred, most of his abilities broken, still he limped across the battlefield, trying until the last to write, to tell his stories. Because that was what he was made for, and he never gave up trying to do what he knew inside was his reason for existence. No longer hailed as a literary hero, he stubbornly labored on until the final critical system failed and the old Bolo at last could rest.

However, when you read these stories, the Bolo is still with us. It may be old now, but despite any rust streaks on its durachrome hull, its hellbores remain forever aimed skyward. The mighty machine with a heart and a mission to fulfill still draws us. Every once in a while, a new publisher and a new editor visit it to buff off the rust and pass the word about its stories, written when the Bolo looked out at the universe and saw adventure and romance and honor. And a new generation of readers drinks them in, because well-written words are immortal. Keith Laumer isn't gone. Here he is, still in his prime, ready for new readers to learn why the Bolo is one of the most memorable characters in science fiction.

BOLO
The Annals of
the Dinochrome Brigade

A Short History of
the Bolo Fighting Machines

The first appearance in history of the concept of the armored vehicle was the use of wooden-shielded war wagons by the reformer John Huss in fifteenth-century Bohemia. Thereafter the idea lapsed—unless one wishes to consider the armored knights of the Middle Ages, mounted on armored warhorses—until the twentieth century. In 1915, during the Great War, the British developed in secrecy a steel-armored motor car; for security reasons during construction it was called a "tank," and the appellation remained in use for the rest of the century. First sent into action at the Somme in A.D. 1916 (BAE 29), the new device was immensely impressive and was soon copied by all belligerents. By Phase Two of the Great War, A.D. 1939-1945, tank corps were a basic element in all modern armies. Quite naturally, great improvements were soon made over the original clumsy, fragile, feeble, and temperamental tank. The British Sheridan and Centurion, the German Tiger, the American Sherman, and the Russian T-34 were all highly potent weapons in their own milieu.

During the long period of cold war following A.D. 1945, development continued, especially in the United States. By 1989 the direct ancestor of the Bolo line had been constructed by the Bolo Division of General Motors. This machine, at one hundred fifty tons almost twice the weight of its Phase Two predecessors, was designated the Bolo Mark I Model B. No Bolo Model A of any mark ever existed, since it was felt that the Ford Motor Company had preempted that designation permanently. The same is true of the name "Model T."

The Mark I was essentially a bigger and better conventional tank, carrying a crew of three and, via power-assisted servos, completely manually operated, with the exception of the capability to perform a number of preset routine functions such as patrol duty with no crew aboard. The Mark II that followed in 1995 was even more highly automated, carrying an onboard fire-control computer and requiring only a single operator. The Mark III of 2020 was considered by some to be almost a step backward, its highly complex controls normally requiring a crew of two, though in an emergency a single experienced man could fight the machine with limited effectiveness. These were by no means negligible weapons systems, their individual firepower exceeding that of a contemporary battalion of heavy infantry, while they were of course correspondingly heavily armored and shielded. The outer durachrome war hull of the Mark III was twenty millimeters thick and capable of withstanding any offensive weapon then known, short of a contact nuclear blast.

The first completely automated Bolo, designed to operate normally without a man aboard, was the landmark Mark XV Model M, originally dubbed *Resartus* for obscure reasons, but later officially named *Stupendous*. This model, first commissioned in the twenty-fifth century, was widely used throughout the Eastern Arm during the Era of Expansion and remained in service on remote worlds for over two centuries, acquiring many improvements in detail along the way while remaining basically unchanged, though increasing sophistication of circuitry and weapons vastly upgraded its effectiveness. The Bolo *Horrendous* Model R, of 2807 was the culmination of this phase of Bolo development, though older models lingered on in the active service of minor powers for centuries.

Thereafter the development of the Mark XVI-XIX consisted largely in further refinement and improvement in detail of the Mark XV. Provision continued to be made for a human occupant, now as a passenger rather than an operator, usually an officer who wished to observe the action at firsthand. Of course, these machines normally went into action under the guidance of individually prepared computer programs, while military regulations continued to require installation of devices for halting or even self-destructing the machine at any time. This latter feature was mainly intended to prevent capture and hostile use of the great machine by an enemy. It was at this time that the first-line Bolos in Terran service were organized into a brigade, known as the Dinochrome Brigade, and deployed as a strategic unit. Tactically the regiment was the basic Bolo unit.

The always-present though perhaps unlikely possibility of capture and use of a Bolo by an enemy was a constant source of anxiety to military leaders and, in time, gave rise to the next and final major advance in Bolo technology: the self-directing (and, quite incidentally, self-aware) Mark XX Model B Bolo *Tremendous.* At this time it was customary to designate each individual unit by a three-letter group indicating hull style, power unit, and main armament. This gave rise to the custom of forming a nickname from the letters, such as "Johnny" from JNY, adding to the tendency to anthropomorphize the great fighting machines.

The Mark XX was at first greeted with little enthusiasm by the High Command, who now professed to believe that an unguided-by-operator Bolo would potentially be capable of running amok and wreaking destruction on its owners. Many observers have speculated by hindsight that a more candid objection would have been that the legitimate area of command function was about to be invaded by mere machinery. Machinery the Bolos were, but never *mere.*

At one time an effort was made to convert a number of surplus Bolos to peacetime use by such modifications as the addition of a soil-moving blade to a Mark XII Bolo WV/I Continental Siege Unit, the installation of seats for four men, and the description of the resulting irresistible force as a "tractor." This idea came to naught, however, since the machines retained their half-megaton/second firepower and were never widely accepted as normal agricultural equipment.

As the great conflict of the post-thirtieth-century era wore on—a period variously known as the Last War and, later, as the Lost War—Bolos of Mark XXVIII and later series were organized into independently operating brigades that did their own strategic as well as tactical planning. Many of these machines still exist in functional condition in out-of-the-way corners of the former Terran Empire. At this time the program of locating and neutralizing these ancient weapons continues.

The Night of the Trolls

It was different this time. There was a dry pain in my lungs, and a deep ache in my bones, and a fire in my stomach that made me want to curl into a ball and mew like a kitten. My mouth tasted as though mice had nested in it, and when I took a deep breath wooden knives twisted in my chest.

I made a mental note to tell Mackenzie a few things about his pet controlled-environment tank—just as soon as I got out of it. I squinted at the over-face panel: air pressure, temperature, humidity, O-level, blood sugar, pulse, and respiration—all okay. That was something. I flipped the intercom key and said, "Okay, Mackenzie, let's have the story. You've got problems ...."

I had to stop to cough. The exertion made my temples pound.

"How long have you birds run this damned exercise?" I called. "I feel lousy. What's going on around here?"

No answer.

This was supposed to be the terminal test series. They couldn't all be out having coffee. The equipment had more bugs than a two-dollar hotel room. I slapped the emergency release lever. Mackenzie wouldn't like it, but to hell with it! From the way I felt, I'd been in the tank for a good long stretch this time—maybe a week or two. And I'd told Ginny it would be a three-dayer at the most. Mackenzie was a great technician, but he had no more human emotions than a used-car salesman. This time I'd tell him.

Relays were clicking, equipment was reacting, the tank cover sliding back. I sat up and swung my legs aside, shivering suddenly.

It was cold in the test chamber. I looked around at the dull gray walls, the data recording cabinets, the wooden desk where Mac sat by the hour rerunning test profiles—

That was funny. The tape reels were empty and the red equipment light was off. I stood, feeling dizzy. Where was Mac? Where were Bonner and Day and Mallon?

"Hey!" I called. I didn't even get a good echo.

Someone must have pushed the button to start my recovery cycle; where were they hiding now? I took a step, tripped over the cables trailing behind me. I unstrapped and pulled the harness off. The effort left me breathing hard. I opened one of the wall lockers; Banner's pressure suit hung limply from the rack beside a rag-festooned coat hanger. I looked in three more lockers. My clothes were missing—even my bathrobe. I also missed the usual bowl of hot soup, the happy faces of the techs, even Mac's sour puss. It was cold and silent and empty here—more like a morgue than a top-priority research center.

I didn't like it. What the hell was going on?

There was a weather suit in the last locker. I put it on, set the temperature control, palmed the door open, and stepped out into the corridor. There were no lights, except for the dim glow of the emergency route indicators. There was a faint, foul odor in the air.

I heard a dry scuttling, saw a flick of movement. A rat the size of a red squirrel sat up on his haunches and looked at me as if I were something to eat. I made a kicking motion and he ran off, but not very far.

My heart was starting to thump a little harder now. The way it does when you begin to realize that something's wrong—bad wrong.

Upstairs in the Admin Section I called again. The echo was a little better here. I went along the corridor strewn with papers, past the open doors of silent rooms. In the Director's office a blackened wastebasket stood in the center of the rug. The air-conditioner intake above the desk was felted over with matted dust nearly an inch thick. There was no use shouting again.

The place was as empty as a robbed grave—except for the rats.

At the end of the corridor, the inner security door stood open. I went through it and stumbled over something. In the faint light, it took me a moment to realize what it was.

He had been an MP, in steel helmet and boots. There was nothing left but crumbled bone and a few scraps of leather and metal. A .38 revolver lay nearby. I picked it up, checked the cylinder, and tucked it in the thigh pocket of the weather suit. For some reason it made me feel a little better.

I went on along B corridor and found the lift door sealed. The emergency stairs were nearby. I went to them and started the two-hundred-foot climb to the surface.

The heavy steel doors at the tunnel had been blown clear.

I stepped past the charred opening, looked out at a low gray sky burning red in the west. Fifty yards away, the five-thousand-gallon water tank lay in a tangle of rusty steel. What had it been? Sabotage, war, revolution—an accident? And where was everybody?

I rested for a while, then went across the innocent-looking fields to the west, dotted with the dummy buildings that were supposed to make the site look from the air like another stretch of farmland complete with barns, sheds, and fences. Beyond the site the town seemed intact: there were lights twinkling here and there, a few smudges of smoke rising. I climbed a heap of rubble for a better view.

Whatever had happened at the site, at least Ginny would be all right—Ginny and Tim. Ginny would be worried sick, after—how long? A month?

Maybe more. There hadn't been much left of that soldier ....

I twisted to get a view to the south, and felt a hollow sensation in my chest. Four silo doors stood open; the Colossus missiles had hit back—at something. I pulled myself up a foot or two higher for a look at the Primary Site. In the twilight the ground rolled smooth and unbroken across the spot where *Prometheus* lay ready in her underground berth. Down below she'd be safe and sound, maybe. She had been built to stand up to the stresses of a direct extrasolar orbital launch; with any luck, a few near misses wouldn't have damaged her.

My arms were aching from the strain of holding on. I climbed down and sat on the ground to get my breath, watching the cold wind worry the dry stalks of dead brush around the fallen tank.

At home, Ginny would be alone, scared, maybe even in serious difficulty. There was no telling how far municipal services had broken down. But before I headed that way, I had to make a quick check on the ship. *Prometheus* was a dream that I—and a lot of others—had lived with for three years. I had to be sure.

I headed toward the pillbox that housed the tunnel head on the off chance that the car might be there.

It was almost dark and the going was tough; the concrete slabs under the sod were tilted and dislocated. Something had sent a ripple across the ground like a stone tossed into a pond.

I heard a sound and stopped dead. There was a clank and rumble from beyond the discolored walls of the blockhouse a hundred yards away. Rusted metal howled; then something as big as a beached freighter moved into view.

Two dull red beams glowing near the top of the high silhouette swung, flashed crimson, and held on me. A siren went off—an ear-splitting whoop! *whoop!* WHOOP!

It was an unmanned Bolo Mark II Combat Unit on automated sentry duty—and its intruder-sensing circuits were tracking me.

The Bolo pivoted heavily; the *whoop! whoop!* sounded again; the robot watchdog was bellowing the alarm.

I felt sweat pop out on my forehead. Standing up to a Mark II Bolo without an electropass was the rough equivalent of being penned in with an ill-tempered dinosaur. I looked toward the Primary blockhouse: too far. The same went for the perimeter fence. My best bet was back to the tunnel mouth. I turned to sprint for it, hooked a foot on a slab and went down hard ....

I got up, my head ringing, tasting blood in my mouth. The chipped pavement seemed to rock under me. The Bolo was coming up fast. Running was no good. I had to have a better idea.

I dropped flat and switched my suit control to maximum insulation.

The silvery surface faded to dull black. A two-foot square of tattered paper fluttered against a projecting edge of concrete; I reached for it, peeled it free, then fumbled with a pocket flap, brought out a permatch, flicked it alight. When the paper was burning well, I tossed it clear. It whirled away a few feet, then caught in a clump of grass.

"Keep moving, damn you!" I whispered. The swearing worked. The gusty wind pushed the paper on. I crawled a few feet and pressed myself into a shallow depression behind the slab. The Bolo churned closer; a loose treadplate was slapping the earth with a rhythmic thud. The burning paper was fifty feet away now, a twinkle of orange light in the deep twilight.

At twenty yards, looming up like a pagoda, the Bolo halted, sat rumbling and swiveling its rust-streaked turret, looking for the radiating source its I-R had first picked up. The flare of the paper caught its electronic attention. The turret swung, then back. It was puzzled. It whooped again, then reached a decision.

Ports snapped open. A volley of antipersonnel slugs whoofed into the target; the scrap of paper disappeared in a gout of tossed dirt.

I hugged the ground like gold lamé hugs a torch singer's hip, and waited; nothing happened. The Bolo sat, rumbling softly to itself. Then I heard another sound over the murmur of the idling engine, a distant roaring, like a flight of low-level bombers. I raised my head half an inch and took a look. There were lights moving beyond the field—the paired beams of a convoy approaching from the town.

The Bolo stirred, moved heavily forward until it towered over me no more than twenty feet away. I saw gun ports open high on the armored facade—the ones that housed the heavy infinite repeaters. Slim black muzzles slid into view, hunted for an instant, then depressed and locked.

They were bearing on the oncoming vehicles that were spreading out now in a loose skirmish line under a roiling layer of dust. The watchdog was getting ready to defend its territory—and I was caught in the middle. A blue-white floodlight lanced out from across the field, glared against the scaled plating of the Bolo. I heard relays click inside the monster fighting machine, and braced myself for the thunder of her battery ....

There was a dry rattle.

The guns traversed, clattering emptily. Beyond the fence the floodlight played for a moment longer against the Bolo, then moved on across the ramp, back, across and back, searching ....

Once more the Bolo fired its empty guns. Its red I-R beams swept the scene again; then relays snicked, the impotent guns retracted, the port covers closed.

Satisfied, the Bolo heaved itself around and moved off, trailing a stink of ozone and ether, the broken tread thumping like a cripple on a stair.

I waited until it disappeared in the gloom two hundred yards away, then cautiously turned my suit control to vent off the heat. Full insulation could boil a man in his own gravy in less than half an hour.

The floodlight had blinked off now. I got to my hands and knees and started toward the perimeter fence. The Bolo's circuits weren't tuned as fine as they should have been; it let me go.

There were men moving in the glare and dust, beyond the rusty lacework that had once been a chain-link fence. They carried guns and stood in tight little groups, staring across toward the blockhouse.

I moved closer, keeping flat and avoiding the avenues of yellowish light thrown by the headlamps of the parked vehicles—halftracks, armored cars, a few light manned tanks.

There was nothing about the look of this crowd that impelled me to leap up and be welcomed. They wore green uniforms, and half of them sported beards. What the hell: had Castro landed in force?

I angled off to the right, away from the big main gate that had been manned day and night by guards with tommy-guns. It hung now by one hinge from a scarred concrete post, under a cluster of dead polyarcs in corroded brackets. The big sign that had read GLENN AEROSPACE CENTER—AUTHORIZED PERSONNEL ONLY lay face down in hip-high underbrush.

More cars were coming up. There was a lot of talk and shouting; a squad of men formed and headed my way, keeping to the outside of the fallen fence.

I was outside the glare of the lights now. I chanced a run for it, got over the sagged wire and across a potholed blacktop road before they reached me. I crouched in the ditch and watched as the detail dropped men in pairs at fifty-yard intervals.

Another five minutes and they would have intercepted me—along with whatever else they were after. I worked my way back across an empty lot and found a strip of lesser underbrush lined with shaggy trees, beneath which a patch of cracked sidewalk showed here and there.

Several things were beginning to be a little clearer now: The person who had pushed the button to bring me out of stasis hadn't been around to greet me, because no one pushed it. The automatics, triggered by some malfunction, had initiated the recovery cycle.

The system's self-contained power unit had been designed to maintain a starship crewman's minimal vital functions indefinitely, at reduced body temperature and metabolic rate. There was no way to tell exactly how long I had been in the tank. From the condition of the fence and the roads, it had been more than a matter of weeks—or even months.

Had it been a year ... or more? I thought of Ginny and the boy, waiting at home—thinking the old man was dead, probably. I'd neglected them before for my work, but not like this ....

Our house was six miles from the base, in the foothills on the other side of town. It was a long walk, the way I felt—but I had to get there.

2

Two hours later I was clear of the town, following the riverbank west.

I kept having the idea that someone was following me. But when I stopped to listen, there was never anything there; just the still, cold night and the frogs, singing away patiently in the low ground to the south.

When the ground began to rise, I left the road and struck off across the open field. I reached a wide street, followed it in a curve that would bring me out at the foot of Ridge Avenue—my street. I could make out the shapes of low, rambling houses now.

It had been the kind of residential section the local Junior Chamber members had hoped to move into some day. Now the starlight that filtered through the cloud cover showed me broken windows, doors that sagged open, automobiles that squatted on flat, dead tires under collapsing car shelters—and here and there a blackened, weed-grown foundation, like a gap in a row of rotting teeth.

The neighborhood wasn't what it had been. How long had I been away? How long …?

I fell down again, hard this time. It wasn't easy getting up. I seemed to weigh a hell of a lot for a guy who hadn't been eating regularly. My breathing was very fast and shallow now, and my skull was getting ready to split and give birth to a live alligator—the ill-tempered kind. It was only a few hundred yards more; but why the hell had I picked a place halfway up a hill?

I heard the sound again—a crackle of dry grass. I got the pistol out and stood flat-footed in the middle of the street, listening hard.

All I heard was my stomach growling. I took the pistol off cock and started off again, stopped suddenly a couple of times to catch him off guard; nothing. I reached the corner of Ridge Avenue, started up the slope. Behind me a stick popped loudly.

I picked that moment to fall down again. Heaped leaves saved me from another skinned knee. I rolled over against a low fieldstone wall and propped myself against it. I had to use both hands to cock the pistol. I stared into the dark, but all I could see were the little lights whirling again. The pistol got heavy; I put it down, concentrated on taking deep breaths and blinking away the fireflies.

I heard footsteps plainly, close by. I shook my head, accidentally banged it against the stone behind me. That helped. I saw him, not over twenty feet away, coming up the hill toward me, a black-haired man with a full beard, dressed in odds and ends of rags and furs, gripping a polished club with a leather thong.

I reached for the pistol, found only leaves, tried again, touched the gun and knocked it away. I was still groping when I heard a scuffle of feet. I swung around, saw a tall, wide figure with a mane of un-trimmed hair.

He hit the bearded man like a pro tackle taking out the practice dummy. They went down together hard and rolled over in a flurry of dry leaves. The cats were fighting over the mouse; that was my signal to leave quietly.

I made one last grab for the gun, found it, got to my feet and staggered off up the grade that seemed as steep now as penthouse rent. And from down slope, I heard an engine gunned, the clash of a heavy transmission that needed adjustment. A spotlight flickered, made shadows dance.

I recognized a fancy wrought-iron fence fronting a vacant lot; that had been the Adams house. Only half a block to go—but I was losing my grip fast. I went down twice more, then gave up and started crawling. The lights were all around now, brighter than ever. My head split open, dropped off, and rolled downhill.

A few more yards and I could let it all go. Ginny would put me in a warm bed, patch up my scratches, and feed me soup. Ginny would ... Ginny ....

I was lying with my mouth full of dead leaves. I heard running feet, yells. An engine idled noisily down the block.

I got my head up and found myself looking at chipped brickwork and the heavy brass hinges from which my front gate had hung. The gate was gone and there was a large chunk of brick missing. Some delivery truck had missed his approach.

I got to my feet, took a couple of steps into deep shadow with feet that felt as though they'd been amputated and welded back on at the ankle. I stumbled, fetched up against something scaled over with rust. I held on, blinked and made out the seeping flank of my brand new '79 Pontiac. There was a crumbled crust of whitish glass lining the brightwork strip that had framed the rear window.

Afire ...?

A footstep sounded behind me, and I suddenly remembered several things, none of them pleasant. I felt for my gun; it was gone. I moved back along the side of the car, tried to hold on.

No use. My arms were like unsuccessful pie crust. I slid down among dead leaves, sat listening to the steps coming closer. They stopped, and through a dense fog that had sprung up suddenly I caught a glimpse of a tall white-haired figure standing over me.

Then the fog closed in and swept everything away.

I lay on my back this time, looking across at the smoky yellow light of a thick brown candle guttering in the draft from a glassless window. In the center of the room a few sticks of damp-looking wood heaped on the cracked asphalt tiles burned with a grayish flame. A thin curl of acrid smoke rose up to stir cobwebs festooned under ceiling beams from which wood veneer had peeled away. Light alloy trusswork showed beneath.

It was a strange scene, but not so strange that I didn't recognize it: it was my own living room—looking a little different than when I had seen it last. The odors were different, too; I picked out mildew, badly cured leather, damp wool, tobacco ….

I turned my head. A yard from the rags I lay on, the white-haired man, looking older than pharaoh, sat sleeping with his back against the wall.

The shotgun was gripped in one big, gnarled hand. His head was tilted back, blue-veined eyelids shut. I sat up, and at my movement his eyes opened.

He lay relaxed for a moment, as though life had to return from some place far away. Then he raised his head. His face was hollow and lined. His white hair was thin. A coarse-woven shirt hung loose across wide shoulders that had been Herculean once. But now Hercules was old, old. He looked at me expectantly.

"Who are you?" I said. "Why did you follow me? What happened to the house? Where's my family? Who owns the bully-boys in green?" My jaw hurt when I spoke. I put my hand up and felt it gingerly.

"You fell," the old man said, in a voice that rumbled like a subterranean volcano.

"The understatement of the year, pop." I tried to get up. Nausea knotted my stomach.

"You have to rest," the old man said, looking concerned. "Before the Baron's men come …." He paused, looking at me as though he expected me to say something profound.

"I want to know where the people are that live here!" My yell came out as weak as church-social punch. "A woman and a boy …."

He was shaking his head. "You have to do something quick. The soldiers will come back, search every house—"

I sat up, ignoring the little men driving spikes into my skull. "I don't give a damn about soldiers! Where's my family? What's happened?" I reached out and gripped his arm. "How long was I down there? What year is this?"

He only shook his head. "Come eat some food. Then I can help you with your plan."

It was no use talking to the old man; he was senile.

I got off the cot. Except for the dizziness and a feeling that my knees were made of papier-mâché, I was all right. I picked up the hand-formed candle, stumbled into the hall.

It was a jumble of rubbish. I climbed through, pushed open the door to my study. There was my desk, the tall bookcase with the glass doors, the gray rug, the easy chair. Aside from a layer of dust and some peeling wallpaper, it looked normal. I flipped the switch. Nothing happened.

"What is that charm?" the old man said behind me. He pointed to the light switch.

"The power's off," I said. "Just habit."

He reached out and flipped the switch up, then down again. "It makes a pleasing sound."

"Yeah." I picked up a book from the desk; it fell apart in my hands.

I went back into the hall, tried the bedroom door, looked in at heaped leaves, the remains of broken furniture, an empty window frame. I went on to the end of the hall and opened the door to the bedroom.

Cold night wind blew through a barricade of broken timbers. The roof had fallen in, and a sixteen-inch tree trunk slanted through the wreckage. The old man stood behind me, watching.

"Where is she, damn you?" I leaned against the door frame to swear and fight off the faintness. "Where's my wife?"

The old man looked troubled. "Come, eat now ...."

"Where is she? Where's the woman who lived here?"

He frowned, shook his head dumbly. I picked my way through the wreckage, stepped out into knee-high brush. A gust blew my candle out. In the dark I stared at my backyard, the crumbled pit that had been the barbecue grill, the tangled thickets that had been rose beds—and a weathered length of boards upended in the earth.

"What the hell's this …?" I fumbled out a permatch, lit my candle, leaned close, and read the crude letters cut into the crumbling wood: VIRGINIA ANNE JACKSON. BORN JAN. 8 1957. KILLED BY THE DOGS WINTER 1992.

3

The Baron's men came twice in the next three days. Each time the old man carried me, swearing but too weak to argue, out to a lean-to of branches and canvas in the woods behind the house. Then he disappeared, to come back an hour or two later and haul me back to my rag bed by the fire.

Three times a day he gave me a tin pan of stew, and I ate it mechanically. My mind went over and over the picture of Ginny, living on for twelve years in the slowly decaying house, and then—

It was too much. There are some shocks the mind refuses.

I thought of the tree that had fallen and crushed the east wing. An elm that size was at least fifty to sixty years old—maybe older. And the only elm on the place had been a two-year sapling. I knew it well; I had planted it.

The date carved on the headboard was 1992. As nearly as I could judge another thirty-five years had passed since then at least. My shipmates—Banner, Day, Mallon—they were all dead, long ago. How had they died? The old man was too far gone to tell me anything useful. Most of my questions produced a shake of the head and a few rumbled words about charms, demons, spells, and the Baron.

"I don't believe in spells," I said. "And I'm not too sure I believe in this Baron. Who is he?"

"The Baron Trollmaster of Filly. He holds all this country—" the old man made a sweeping gesture with his arm—"all the way to Jersey."

"Why was he looking for me? What makes me important?"

"You came from the Forbidden Place. Everyone heard the cries of the Lesser Troll that stands guard over the treasure there. If the Baron can learn your secrets of power—"

"Troll, hell! That's nothing but a Bolo on automatic!"

"By any name every man dreads the monster. A man who walks in its shadow has much *mana*. But the others—the ones that run in a pack like dogs—would tear you to pieces for a demon if they could lay hands on you."

"You saw me back there. Why didn't you give me away? And why are you taking care of me now?"

He shook his head—the all-purpose answer to any question.

I tried another tack: "Who was the rag man you tackled just outside? Why was he laying for me?"

The old man snorted. "Tonight the dogs will eat him. But forget that. Now we have to talk about your plan—"

"I've got about as many plans as the senior boarder in death row. I don't know if you know it, old timer, but somebody slid the world out from under me while I wasn't looking."

The old man frowned. I had the thought that I wouldn't like to have him mad at me, for all his white hair ....

He shook his head. "You must understand what I tell you. The soldiers of the Baron will find you someday. If you are to break the spell—"

"Break the spell, eh?" I snorted. "I think I get the idea, pop. You've got it in your head that I'm valuable property of some kind. You figure I can use my supernatural powers to take over this menagerie—and you'll be in on the ground floor. Well, listen, you old idiot! I spent sixty years—maybe more—in a stasis tank two hundred feet underground. My world died while I was down there. This Baron of yours seems to own everything now. If you think I'm going to get myself shot bucking him, forget it!"

The old man didn't say anything.

"Things don't seem to be broken up much," I went on. "It must have been gas, or germ warfare—or fallout. Damn few people around. You're still able to live on what you can loot from stores; automobiles are still sitting where they were the day the world ended. How old were you when it happened, pop? The war, I mean. Do you remember it?"

He shook his head. "The world has always been as it is now."

"What year were you born?"

He scratched at his white hair. "I knew the number once. But I've forgotten."

"I guess the only way I'll find out how long I was gone is to saw that damned elm in two and count the rings—but even that wouldn't help much; I don't know when it blew over. Never mind. The important thing now is to talk to this Baron of yours. Where does he stay?"

The old man shook his head violently. "If the Baron lays his hands on you, he'll wring the secrets from you on the rack! I know his ways. For five years I was a slave in the palace stables."

"If you think I'm going to spend the rest of my days in this rat nest, you get another guess on the house! This Baron has tanks, an army. He's kept a little technology alive. That's the outfit for me—not this garbage detail! Now, where's this place of his located?"

"The guards will shoot you on sight like a pack-dog!"

"There has to be a way to get to him, old man! Think!"

The old head was shaking again. "He fears assassination. You can never approach him ...." He brightened. "Unless you know a spell of power?"

I chewed my lip. "Maybe I do at that. You wanted me to have a plan. I think I feel one coming on. Have you got a map?"

He pointed to the desk beside me. I tried the drawers, found mice, roaches, moldy money—and a stack of folded maps. I opened one carefully; faded ink on yellowed paper falling apart at the creases. The legend in the corner read: "PENNSYLVANIA 40M:1. Copyright 1970 ESSO Corporation."

"This will do, pop," I said. "Now, tell me all you can about this Baron of yours."

"You'll destroy him?"

"I haven't even met the man."

"He is evil."

"I don't know; he owns an army. That makes up for a lot ...."

After three more days of rest and the old man's stew I was back to normal—or near enough. I had the old man boil me a tub of water for a bath and a shave. I found a serviceable pair of synthetic-fiber long johns in a chest of drawers, pulled them on and zipped the weather suit over them, then buckled on the holster I had made from a tough plastic.

"That completes my preparations, pop," I said. "It'll be dark in another half hour. Thanks for everything."

He got to his feet, a worried look on his lined face, like a father the first time Junior asks for the car.

"The Baron's men are everywhere."

"If you want to help, come along and back me up with that shotgun of yours." I picked it up. "Have you got any shells for this thing?"

He smiled, pleased now. "There are shells—but the magic is gone from many."

"That's the way magic is, pop. It goes out of things before you notice."

"Will you destroy the Great Troll now?"

"My motto is let sleeping trolls lie. I'm just paying a social call on the Baron."

The joy ran out of his face like booze from a dropped jug.

"Don't take it so hard, old timer. I'm not the fairy prince you were expecting. But I'll take care of you—if I make it."

I waited while he pulled on a moth-eaten mackinaw. He took the shotgun and checked the breech, then looked at me.

"I'm ready," he said.

"Yeah," I said. "Let's go …."

The Baronial palace was a forty-story slab of concrete and glass that had been known in my days as the Hilton Garden East. We made it in three hours of groping across country in the dark, at the end of which I was puffing but still on my feet. We moved out from the cover of the trees and looked across a dip in the ground at the lights, incongruously cheerful in the ravaged valley.

"The gates are there—" the old man pointed—"guarded by the Great Troll."

"Wait a minute. I thought the Troll was the Bolo back at the Site."

"That's the Lesser Troll. This is the Great One."

I selected a few choice words and muttered them to myself. "It would have saved us some effort if you'd mentioned this troll a little sooner, old timer. I'm afraid I don't have any spells that will knock out a Mark II, once it's got its dander up."

He shook his head. "It lies under enchantment. I remember the day when it came, throwing thunderbolts. Many men were killed. Then the Baron commanded it to stand at his gates to guard him."

"How long ago was this, old timer?"

He worked his lips over the question. "Long ago," he said finally. "Many winters."

"Let's go take a look."

We picked our way down the slope, came up along a rutted dirt road to the dark line of trees that rimmed the palace grounds. The old man touched my arm.

"Softly here. Maybe the Troll sleeps lightly ...."

I went the last few yards, eased around a brick column with a dead lantern on top, stared across fifty yards of waist-high brush at a dark silhouette outlined against the palace lights.

Cables, stretched from trees outside the circle of weeds, support-ed a weathered tarp which drooped over the Bolo. The wreckage of a helicopter lay like a crumpled dragonfly at the far side of the ring. Nearer, fragments of a heavy car chassis lay scattered. The old man hovered at my shoulder.

"It looks as though the gate is off limits," I hissed. "Let's try far-ther along."

He nodded. "No one passes here. There is a second gate, there." He pointed. "But there are guards."

"Let's climb the wall between gates."

"There are sharp spikes on top of the wall. But I know a place, farther on, where the spikes have been blunted."

"Lead on, pop."

Half an hour of creeping through wet brush brought us to the spot we were looking for. It looked to me like any other stretch of eight-foot masonry wall overhung with wet poplar trees.

"I'll go first," the old man said, "to draw the attention of the guard."

"Then who's going to boost me up? I'll go first."

He nodded, cupped his hands and lifted me as easily as a sailor lifting a beer glass. Pop was old—but he was nobody's softie.

I looked around, then crawled up, worked my way over the corroded spikes, dropped down on the lawn.

Immediately I heard a crackle of brush. A man stood up not ten feet away. I lay flat in the dark trying to look like something that had been there a long time ....

I heard another sound, a thump and a crashing of brush. The man before me turned, disappeared in the darkness. I heard him beating his way through shrubbery; then he called out, got an answering shout from the distance.

I didn't loiter. I got to my feet and made a sprint for the cover of the trees along the drive.

4

Flat on the wet ground, under the wind-whipped branches of an ornamental cedar, I blinked the fine misty rain from my eyes, waiting for the halfhearted alarm behind me to die down.

There were a few shouts, some sounds of searching among the shrubbery. It was a bad night to be chasing imaginary intruders in the Baronial grounds. In five minutes all was quiet again.

I studied the view before me. The tree under which I lay was one of a row lining a drive. It swung in a graceful curve, across a smooth half-mile of dark lawn, to the tower of light that was the palace of the Baron of Filly. The silhouetted figures of guards and late-arriving guests moved against the gleam from the colonnaded entrance. On a terrace high above, dancers twirled under colored lights. The faint glow of the repellor field kept the cold rain at a distance. In a lull in the wind, I heard music, faintly. The Baron's weekly grand ball was in full swing.

I saw shadows move across the wet gravel before me, then heard the purr of an engine. I hugged the ground and watched a long svelte Mercedes—about an '88 model, I estimated—barrel past.

The mob in the city ran in packs like dogs, but the Baron's friends did a little better for themselves.

I got to my feet and moved off toward the palace, keeping well in the shadows. When the drive swung to the right to curve across in front of the building, I left it, went to hands and knees, and followed a trimmed privet hedge past dark rectangles of formal garden to the edge of a secondary pond of light from the garages. I let myself down on my belly and watched the shadows that moved on the graveled drive.

There seemed to be two men on duty—no more. Waiting around wouldn't improve my chances. I got to my feet, stepped out into the drive, and walked openly around the corner of the gray fieldstone building into the light.

A short, thickset man in greasy Baronial green looked at me incuriously. My weather suit looked enough like ordinary coveralls to get me by—at least for a few minutes. A second man, tilted back against the wall in a wooden chair, didn't even turn his head.

"Hey!" I called. "You birds got a three-ton jack I can borrow?"

Shorty looked me over sourly. "Who you drive for, Mac?"

"The High Duke of Jersey. Flat. Left rear. On a night like this. Some luck."

"The Jersey can't afford a jack?"

I stepped over to the short man, prodded him with a forefinger. "He could buy you and gut you on the altar any Saturday night of the week, low-pockets. And he'd get a kick out of doing it. He's like that."

"Can't a guy crack a harmless joke without somebody talks about altar-bait? You wanna jack, take a jack."

The man in the chair opened one eye and looked me over. "How long you on the Jersey payroll?" he growled.

"Long enough to know who handles the rank between Jersey and Filly." I yawned, looked around the wide, cement-floored garage, glanced over the four heavy cars with the Filly crest on their sides.

"Where's the kitchen? I'm putting a couple of hot coffees under my belt before I go back out into that."

"Over there. A flight up and to your left. Tell the cook Pintsy invited you."

"I tell him Jersey sent me, low-pockets." I moved off in a dead silence, opened the door and stepped up into spicy-scented warmth.

A deep carpet—even here—muffled my footsteps. I could hear the clash of pots and crockery from the kitchen a hundred feet distant along the hallway. I went along to a deep-set doorway ten feet from the kitchen, tried the knob, and looked into a dark room. I pushed the door shut and leaned against it, watching the kitchen. Through the woodwork I could feel the thump of the bass notes from the orchestra blasting away three flights up. The odors of food—roast fowl, baked ham, grilled horsemeat—curled under the kitchen door and wafted under my nose. I pulled my belt up a notch and tried to swallow the dryness in my throat. The old man had fed me a half a gallon of stew before we left home, but I was already working up a fresh appetite.

Five slow minutes passed. Then the kitchen door swung open and a tall round-shouldered fellow with a shiny bald scalp stepped into view, a tray balanced on the spread fingers of one hand. He turned, the black tails of his cutaway swirling, called something behind him, and started past me. I stepped out, clearing my throat. He shied, whirled to face me. He was good at his job: the two dozen tiny glasses on the tray stood fast. He blinked, got an indignant remark ready—

I showed him the knife the old man had lent me—a bonehandled job with a six-inch switchblade. "Make a sound and I'll cut your throat," I said softly. "Put the tray on the floor."

He started to back. I brought the knife up. He took a good look, licked his lips, crouched quickly, and put the tray down.

"Turn around."

I stepped in and chopped him at the base of the neck with the edge of my hand. He folded like a two-dollar umbrella.

I wrestled the door open and dumped him inside, paused a moment to listen. All quiet. I worked his black coat and trousers off, unhooked the stiff white dickey and tie. He snored softly. I pulled the clothes on over the weather suit. They were a fair fit. By the light of my pencil flash I cut down a heavy braided cord hanging by a high window, used it to truss the waiter's hands and feet together behind him. There was a small closet opening off the room. I put him in it, closed the door, and stepped back into the hall. Still quiet. I tried one of the drinks. It wasn't bad.

I took another, then picked up the tray and followed the sounds of music.

The grand ballroom was a hundred yards long, fifty wide, with walls of rose, gold, and white, banks of high windows hung with crimson velvet, a vaulted ceiling decorated with cherubs, and a polished acre of floor on which gaudily gowned and uniformed couples moved in time to the heavy beat of the traditional foxtrot. I moved slowly along the edge of the crowd, looking for the Baron.

A hand caught my arm and hauled me around. A glass fell off my tray, smashed on the floor.

A dapper little man in black and white headwaiter's uniform glared up at me.

"What do you think you're doing, cretin?" he hissed. "That's the genuine ancient stock you're slopping on the floor." I looked around quickly; no one else seemed to be paying any attention.

"Where are you from?" he snapped. I opened my mouth—

"Never mind, you're all the same." He waggled his hands disgustedly. "The field hands they send me—a disgrace to the Black. Now, you! Stand up! Hold your tray proudly, gracefully! Step along daintily, not like a knight taking the field! and pause occasionally—just on the chance that some noble guest might wish to drink."

"You bet, pal," I said. I moved on, paying a little more attention to my waiting. I saw plenty of green uniforms; pea green, forest green, emerald green—but they were all hung with braid and medals. According to pop, the Baron affected a spartan simplicity. The diffidence of absolute power.

There were high white and gold doors every few yards along the side of the ballroom. I spotted one standing open and sidled toward it. It wouldn't hurt to reconnoiter the area.

Just beyond the door, a very large sentry in a bottle-green uniform almost buried under gold braid moved in front of me. He was dressed like a toy soldier, but there was nothing playful about the way he snapped his power gun to the ready. I winked at him.

"Thought you boys might want a drink," I hissed. "Good stuff."

He looked at the tray, licked his lips. "Get back in there, you fool," he growled. "You'll get us both hanged."

"Suit yourself, pal." I backed out. Just before the door closed between us, he lifted a glass off the tray.

I turned, almost collided with a long lean cookie in a powder-blue outfit complete with dress saber, gold frogs, leopard-skin facings, a pair of knee-length white gloves looped under an epaulette, a pistol in a fancy holster, and an eighteen-inch swagger stick. He gave me the kind of look old maids give sin.

"Look where you're going, swine," he said in a voice like a pine board splitting.

"Have a drink, admiral," I suggested.

He lifted his upper lip to show me a row of teeth that hadn't had their annual trip to the dentist lately. The ridges along each side of his mouth turned greenish white. He snatched for the gloves on his shoulder, fumbled them; they slapped the floor beside me.

"I'd pick those up for you, boss," I said, "but I've got my tray ...."

He drew a breath between his teeth, chewed it into strips, and snorted it back at me, then snapped his fingers and pointed with his stick toward the door behind me.

"Through there, instantly!" It didn't seem like the time to argue; I pulled it open and stepped through.

The guard in green ducked his glass and snapped to attention when he saw the baby-blue outfit. My new friend ignored him, made a curt gesture to me. I got the idea, trailed along the wide, high, gloomy corridor to a small door, pushed through it into a well-lit tile-walled latrine. A big-eyed slave in white ducks stared.

Blue-boy jerked his head. "Get out!" The slave scuttled away. Blue-boy turned to me.

"Strip off your jacket, slave! Your owner has neglected to teach you discipline."

I looked around quickly, saw that we were alone.

"Wait a minute while I put the tray down, corporal," I said. "We don't want to waste any of the good stuff." I turned to put the tray on a soiled linen bin, caught a glimpse of motion in the mirror.

I ducked, and the nasty-looking little leather quirt whistled past my ear, slammed against the edge of a marble-topped lavatory with a crack like a pistol shot. I dropped the tray, stepped in fast and threw a left to Blue-boy's jaw that bounced his head against the tiled wall.

I followed up with a right to the belt buckle, then held him up as he bent over, gagging, and hit him hard under the ear.

I hauled him into a booth, propped him up and started shedding the waiter's blacks.

5

I left him on the floor wearing my old suit, and stepped out into the hall.

I liked the feel of his pistol at my hip. It was an old-fashioned .38, the same model I favored. The blue uniform was a good fit, what with the weight I'd lost. Blue-boy and I had something in common after all.

The latrine attendant goggled at me. I grimaced like a quadruple amputee trying to scratch his nose and jerked my head toward the door I had come out of. I hoped the gesture would look familiar.

"Truss that mad dog and throw him outside the gates," I snarled. I stamped off down the corridor, trying to look mad enough to discourage curiosity.

Apparently it worked. Nobody yelled for the cops.

I reentered the ballroom by another door, snagged a drink off a passing tray, checked over the crowd. I saw two more powder-blue getups, so I wasn't unique enough to draw special attention. I made a mental note to stay well away from my comrades in blue. I blended with the landscape, chatting and nodding and not neglecting my drinking, working my way toward a big arched doorway on the other side of the room that looked like the kind of entrance the head man might use. I didn't want to meet him. Not yet. I just wanted to get him located before I went any further.

A passing wine slave poured a full inch of genuine ancient stock into my glass, ducked his head, and moved on. I gulped it like sour bar whiskey. My attention was elsewhere.

A flurry of activity near the big door indicated that maybe my guess had been accurate. Potbellied officials were forming up in a sort of reception line near the big double door. I started to drift back into the rear rank, bumped against a fat man in medals and a sash who glared, fingered a monocle with a plump ring-studded hand, and said, "Suggest you take your place, colonel," in a suety voice.

I must have looked doubtful, because he bumped me with his paunch, and growled, "Foot of the line! Next to the Equerry, you idiot." He elbowed me aside and waddled past.

I took a step after him, reached out with my left foot, and hooked his shiny black boot. He leaped forward, off balance, medals jangling. I did a fast fade while he was still groping for his monocle, eased into a spot at the end of the line.

The conversation died away to a nervous murmur. The doors swung back and a pair of guards with more trimmings than a phony stock certificate stamped into view, wheeled to face each other, and presented arms—chrome-plated automatic rifles, in this case. A dark-faced man with thinning gray hair, a pug nose, and a trimmed gray Vandyke came into view, limping slightly from a stiffish knee.

His unornamented gray outfit made him as conspicuous in this gathering as a crane among peacocks. He nodded perfunctorily to left and right, coming along between the waiting rows of flunkeys, who snapped-to as he came abreast, wilted, and let out sighs behind him. I studied him closely. He was fifty, give or take the age of a bottle of second-rate bourbon, with the weather-beaten complexion of a former outdoor man and the same look of alertness grown bored that a rattlesnake farmer develops—just before the fatal bite.

He looked up and caught my eye on him, and for a moment I thought he was about to speak. Then he went on past.

At the end of the line he turned abruptly and spoke to a man who hurried away. Then he engaged in conversation with a cluster of head-bobbing guests.

I spent the next fifteen minutes casually getting closer to the door nearest the one the Baron had entered by. I looked around; nobody was paying any attention to me. I stepped past a guard who presented arms. The door closed softly, cutting off the buzz of talk and the worst of the music.

I went along to the end of the corridor. From the transverse hall, a grand staircase rose in a sweep of bright chrome and pale wood. I didn't know where it led, but it looked right. I headed for it, moving along briskly like a man with important business in mind and no time for light chitchat.

Two flights up, in a wide corridor of muted lights, deep carpets, brocaded wall hangings, mirrors, urns, and an odor of expensive tobacco and *cuir russe,* a small man in black bustled from a side corridor. He saw me. He opened his mouth, closed it, half turned away, then swung back to face me. I recognized him; he was the headwaiter who had pointed out the flaws in my waiting style half an hour earlier.

"Here—" he started.

I chopped him short with a roar of what I hoped was authentic upper-crust rage.

"Direct me to his Excellency's apartments, scum! And thank your guardian imp I'm in too great haste to cane you for the insolent look about you!"

He went pale, gulped hard, and pointed. I snorted and stamped past him down the turning he had indicated.

This was Baronial country, all right. A pair of guards stood at the far end of the corridor.

I'd passed half a dozen with no more than a click of heels to indicate they saw me. These two shouldn't be any different—and it wouldn't look good if I turned and started back at sight of them. The first rule of the gate-crasher is to look as if you belong where you are.

I headed in their direction.

When I was fifty feet from them they both shifted rifles—not to present-arms position, but at the ready. The nickel-plated bayonets were aimed right at me. It was no time for me to look doubtful; I kept on coming. At twenty feet, I heard their rifle bolts snick home. I could see the expressions on their faces now; they looked as nervous as a couple of teenage sailors on their first visit to a joyhouse.

"Point those butter knives into the corner, you banana-fingered cotton choppers!" I said, looking bored, and didn't waver. I unlimbered my swagger stick and slapped my gloved hand with it, letting them think it over. The gun muzzles dropped—just slightly. I followed up fast.

"Which is the anteroom to the Baron's apartments?" I demanded.

"Uh ... this here is his Excellency's apartments, sir, but—"

"Never mind the lecture, you milk-faced fool," I cut in. "Which is the anteroom, damn you!"

"We got orders, sir. Nobody's to come closer than that last door back there."

"We got orders to shoot," the other interrupted. He was a little older—maybe twenty-two. I turned on him.

"I'm waiting for an answer to a question!"

"Sir, the Articles—"

I narrowed my eyes. "I think you'll find paragraph Two B covers Special Cosmic Top Secret Couriers. When you go off duty, report yourselves on punishment. Now, the anteroom! And be quick about it!"

The bayonets were sagging now. The younger of the two licked his lips. "Sir, we never been inside. We don't know how it's laid out in there. If the colonel wants to just take a look ...."

The other guard opened his mouth to say something. I didn't wait to find out what it was. I stepped between them, muttering something about bloody recruits and important messages, and worked the fancy handle on the big gold-and-white door. I paused to give the two sentries a hard look.

"I hope I don't have to remind you that any mention of the movements of a Cosmic Courier is punishable by slow death. Just forget you ever saw me." I went on in and closed the door without waiting to catch the reaction to that one.

The Baron had done well by himself in the matter of decor. The room I was in—a sort of lounge-cum-bar—was paved in two-inch-deep nylon fuzz, the color of a fog at sea, that foamed up at the edges against walls of pale-blue brocade with tiny yellow flowers. The bar was a teak log split down the middle and polished. The glasses sitting on it were like tissue paper engraved with patterns of nymphs and satyrs. Subdued light came from somewhere, along with a faint melody that seemed to speak of youth, long ago.

I went on into the room. I found more soft light, the glow of hand-rubbed rare woods, rich fabrics, and wide windows with a view of dark night sky. The music was coming from a long, low, built-in speaker with a lamp, a heavy crystal ashtray, and a display of hothouse roses. There was a scent in the air. Not the *cuir russe* and Havana leaf I'd smelled in the hall, but a subtler perfume.

I turned and looked into the eyes of a girl with long black lashes. Smooth black hair came down to bare shoulders. An arm as smooth and white as whipped cream was draped over a chair back, the hand holding an eight-inch cigarette holder and sporting a diamond as inconspicuous as a chrome-plated hubcap.

"You must want something pretty badly," she murmured, batting her eyelashes at me. I could feel the breeze at ten feet. I nodded. Under the circumstances that was about the best I could do.

"What could it be," she mused, "that's worth being shot for?" Her voice was like the rest of her: smooth, polished and relaxed—and with plenty of moxie held in reserve. She smiled casually, drew on her cigarette, tapped ashes onto the rug.

"Something bothering you, colonel?" she inquired. "You don't seem talkative."

"I'll do my talking when the Baron arrives," I said.

"In that case, Jackson," said a husky voice behind me, "you can start any time you like."

I held my hands clear of my body and turned around slowly—just in case there was a nervous gun aimed at my spine. The Baron was standing near the door, unarmed, relaxed. There were no guards in sight. The girl looked mildly amused. I put my hand on the pistol butt.

"How do you know my name?" I asked.

The Baron waved toward a chair. "Sit down, Jackson," he said, almost gently. "You've had a tough time of it—but you're all right now." He walked past me to the bar, poured out two glasses, turned, and offered me one. I felt a little silly standing there fingering the gun; I went over and took the drink.

"To the old days." The Baron raised his glass.

I drank. It was the genuine ancient stock, all right. "I asked you how you knew my name," I said.

"That's easy. I used to know you."

He smiled faintly. There was something about his face ….

"You look well in the uniform of the Penn dragoons," he said. "Better than you ever did in Aerospace blue."

"Good God!" I said. "Toby Mallon!"

He ran a hand over his bald head. "A little less hair on top, plus a beard as compensation, a few wrinkles, a slight pot. Oh, I've changed, Jackson."

"I had it figured as close to eighty years," I said. "The trees, the condition of the buildings—"

"Not far off the mark. Seventy-eight years this spring."

"You're a well-preserved hundred and ten, Toby."

He nodded. "I know how you feel. Rip Van Winkle had nothing on us."

"Just one question, Toby. The men you sent out to pick me up seemed more interested in shooting than talking. I'm wondering why."

Mallon threw out his hands. "A little misunderstanding, Jackson. You made it; that's all that counts. Now that you're here, we've got some planning to do together. I've had it tough these last twenty years. I started off with nothing: a few hundred scavengers living in the ruins, hiding out every time Jersey or Dee-Cee raided for supplies. I built an organization, started a systematic salvage operation. I saved everything the rats and the weather hadn't gotten to, spruced up my palace here, and stocked it. It's a rich province, Jackson—"

"And now you own it all. Not bad, Toby."

"They say knowledge is power. I had the knowledge."

I finished my drink and put the glass on the bar.

"What's this planning you say we have to do?"

Mallon leaned back on one elbow.

"Jackson, it's been a long haul—alone. It's good to see an old shipmate. But we'll dine first."

"I might manage to nibble a little something. Say a horse, roasted whole. Don't bother to remove the saddle."

He laughed. "First we eat," he said. "Then we conquer the world."

6

I squeezed the last drop from the Beaujolais bottle and watched the girl, whose name was Renada, hold a light for the cigar Mallon had taken from a silver box. My blue mess jacket and holster hung over the back of the chair. Everything was cozy now.

"Time for business, Jackson," Mallon said. He blew out smoke and looked at me through it. "How did things look—inside?"

"Dusty. But intact, below ground level. Upstairs, there's blast damage and weathering. I don't suppose it's changed much since you came out twenty years ago. As far as I could tell, the Primary Site is okay."

Mallon leaned forward. "Now, you made it out past the Bolo. How did it handle itself? Still fully functional?"

I sipped my wine, thinking over my answer, remembering the Bolo's empty guns ….

"It damn near gunned me down. It's getting a little old and it can't see as well as it used to, but it's still a tough baby."

Mallon swore suddenly. "It was Mackenzie's idea. A last-minute move when the tech crews had to evacuate. It was a dusting job, you know."

"I hadn't heard. How did you find out all this?"

Mallon shot me a sharp look. "There were still a few people around who'd been in it. But never mind that. What about the Supply Site? That's what we're interested in. Fuel, guns, even some nuclear stuff. Heavy equipment; there's a couple more Bolos, mothballed, I understand. Maybe we'll even find one or two of the Colossus missiles still in their silos. I made an air recon a few years back before my chopper broke down—"

"I think two silo doors are still in place. But why the interest in armament?"

Mallon snorted. "You've got a few things to learn about the setup, Jackson. I need that stuff. If I hadn't lucked into a stock of weapons and ammo in the armory cellar, Jersey would be wearing the spurs in my palace right now!"

I drew on my cigar and let the silence stretch out.

"You said something about conquering the world, Toby. I don't suppose by any chance you meant that literally?"

Mallon stood up, his closed fists working like a man crumpling unpaid bills. "They all want what I've got! They're all waiting." He walked across the room, back. "I'm ready to move against them now! I can put four thousand trained men in the field—"

"Let's get a couple of things straight, Mallon," I cut in. "You've got the natives fooled with this Baron routine. But don't try it on me.

Maybe it was even necessary once; maybe there's an excuse for some of the stories I've heard. That's over now. I'm not interested in tribal warfare or gang rumbles. I need—"

"Better remember who's running things here, Jackson!" Mallon snapped. "It's not what you need that counts." He took another turn up and down the room, then stopped, facing me.

"Look, Jackson. I know how to get around in this jungle; you don't. If I hadn't spotted you and given some orders, you'd have been gunned down before you'd gone ten feet past the ballroom door."

"Why'd you let me in? I might've been gunning for you."

"You wanted to see the Baron alone. That suited me, too. If word got out—" He broke off, cleared his throat. "Let's stop wrangling, Jackson. We can't move until the Bolo guarding the site has been neutralized. There's only one way to do that: knock it out! And the only thing that can knock out a Bolo is another Bolo."

"So?"

"I've got another Bolo, Jackson. It's been covered, maintained. It can go up against the Troll—" He broke off, laughed shortly. "That's what the mob called it."

"You could have done that years ago. Where do I come in?"

"You're checked out on a Bolo, Jackson. You know something about this kind of equipment."

"Sure. So do you."

"I never learned," he said shortly.

"Who's kidding who, Mallon? We all took the same orientation course less than a month ago—"

"For me it's been a long month. Let's say I've forgotten."

"You parked that Bolo at your front gate and then forgot how you did it, eh?"

"Nonsense. It's always been there."

I shook my head. "I know different."

Mallon looked wary. "Where'd you get that idea?"

"Somebody told me."

Mallon ground his cigar out savagely on the damask cloth. "You'll point the scum out to me!"

"I don't give a damn whether you moved it or not. Anybody with your training can figure out the controls of a Bolo in half an hour—"

"Not well enough to take on the Tr—another Bolo."

I took a cigar from the silver box, picked up the lighter from the table, turned the cigar in the flame. Suddenly it was very quiet in the room.

I looked across at Mallon. He held out his hand.

"I'll take that," he said shortly.

I blew out smoke, squinted through it at Mallon. He sat with his hand out, waiting. I looked down at the lighter.

It was a heavy windproof model with embossed Aerospace wings. I turned it over. Engraved letters read: *Lieut. Commander Don G. Banner, USAF.* I looked up. Renada sat quietly, holding my pistol trained dead on my belt buckle.

"I'm sorry you saw that," Mallon said. "It could cause misunderstandings."

"Where's Banner?"

"He … died. I told you—"

"You told me a lot of things, Toby. Some of them might even be true. Did you make him the same offer you've made me?"

Mallon darted a look at Renada. She sat holding the pistol, looking at me distantly, without expression.

"You've got the wrong idea, Jackson—" Mallon started.

"You and he came out about the same time," I said. "Or maybe you got the jump on him by a few days. It must have been close; otherwise you'd never have taken him. Don was a sharp boy."

"You're out of your mind!" Mallon snapped. "Why, Banner was my friend!"

"Then why do you get nervous when I find his lighter on your table? There could be ten perfectly harmless explanations."

"I don't make explanations," Mallon said flatly.

"That attitude is hardly the basis for a lasting partnership, Toby. I have an unhappy feeling there's something you're not telling me."

Mallon pulled himself up in the chair. "Look here, Jackson. We've no reason to fall out. There's plenty for both of us—and one day I'll be needing a successor. It was too bad about Banner, but that's ancient history now. Forget it. I want you with me, Jackson! Together we can rule the Atlantic seaboard—or even more!"

I drew on my cigar, looking at the gun in Renada's hand. "You hold the aces, Toby. Shooting me would be no trick at all."

"There's no trick involved, Jackson!" Mallon snapped. "After all," he went on, almost wheedling now, "we're old friends. I want to give you a break, share with you—"

"I don't think I'd trust him if I were you, Mr. Jackson," Renada's quiet voice cut in. I looked at her. She looked back calmly. "You're more important to him than you think."

"That's enough, Renada," Mallon barked. "Go to your room at once."

"Not just yet, Toby," she said. "I'm also curious about how Commander Banner died." I looked at the gun in her hand.

It wasn't pointed at me now. It was aimed at Mallon's chest.

Mallon sat sunk deep in his chair, looking at me with eyes like a python with a bellyache. "You're fools, both of you," he grated. "I gave you everything, Renada. I raised you like my own daughter. And you, Jackson. You could have shared with me—all of it."

"I don't need a share of your delusions, Toby. I've got a set of my own. But before we go any further, let's clear up a few points. Why haven't you been getting any mileage out of your tame Bolo? And what makes me important in the picture?"

"He's afraid of the Bolo machine," Renada said. "There's a spell on it which prevents men from approaching—even the Baron."

"Shut your mouth, you fool!" Mallon choked on his fury. I tossed the lighter in my hand and felt a smile twitching at my mouth.

"So Don was too smart for you after all. He must have been the one who had control of the Bolo. I suppose you called for a truce, and then shot him out from under the white flag. But he fooled you. He plugged a command into the Bolo's circuits to fire on anyone who came close—unless he was Banner."

"You're crazy!"

"It's close enough. You can't get near the Bolo. Right? And after twenty years, the bluff you've been running on the other Barons with your private troll must be getting a little thin. Any day now one of them may decide to try you."

Mallon twisted his face in what may have been an attempt at a placating smile. "I won't argue with you, Jackson. You're right about the command circuit. Banner set it up to fire an antipersonnel blast at anyone coming within fifty yards. He did it to keep the mob from tampering with the machine. But there's a loophole. It wasn't only

Banner who could get close. He set it up to accept any of the *Prometheus* crew—except me. He hated me. It was a trick to try to get me killed."

"So you're figuring I'll step in and defuse her for you, eh, Toby? Well, I'm sorry as hell to disappoint you, but somehow in the confusion I left my electropass behind."

Mallon leaned toward me. "I told you we need each other, Jackson: I've got your pass. Yours and all the others. Renada, hand me my black box." She rose and moved across to the desk, holding the gun on Mallon—and on me, too, for that matter.

"Where'd you get my pass, Mallon?"

"Where do you think? They're the duplicates from the vault in the old command block. I knew one day one of you would come out. I'll tell you, Jackson, it's been hell, waiting all these years—and hoping. I gave orders that any time the Great Troll bellowed, the mob was to form up and stop anybody who came out. I don't know how you got through them …."

"I was too slippery for them. Besides," I added, "I met a friend."

"A friend? Who's that?"

"An old man who thought I was Prince Charming, come to wake everybody up. He was nuts. But he got me through."

Renada came back, handed me a square steel box. "Let's have the key, Mallon," I said. He handed it over. I opened the box, sorted through half a dozen silver-dollar-sized ovals of clear plastic, lifted one out.

"Is it a magical charm?" Renada asked, sounding awed. She didn't seem so sophisticated now—but I liked her better human.

"Just a synthetic crystalline plastic, designed to resonate to a pattern peculiar to my EEG," I said. "It amplifies the signal and gives off a characteristic emission that the psychotronic circuit in the Bolo picks up."

"That's what I thought. Magic."

"Call it magic, then, kid." I dropped the electropass in my pocket, stood and looked at Renada. "I don't doubt that you know how to use that gun, honey, but I'm leaving now. Try not to shoot me."

"You're a fool if you try it," Mallon barked. "If Renada doesn't shoot you, my guards will. And even if you made it, you'd still need me!"

"I'm touched by your concern, Toby. Just why do I need you?"

"You wouldn't get past the first sentry post without help, Jackson. These people know me as the Trollmaster. They're in awe of me—of my *mana*. But together—we can get to the controls of the Bolo, then use it to knock out the sentry machine at the Site—"

"Then what? With an operating Bolo I don't need anything else. Better improve the picture, Toby. I'm not impressed."

He wet his lips.

"It's *Prometheus,* do you understand? She's stocked with everything from Browning needlers to Norge stunners. Tools, weapons, instruments. And the power plants alone."

"I don't need needlers if I own a Bolo, Toby."

Mallon used some profanity. "You'll leave your liver and lights on the palace altar, Jackson. I promise you that!"

"Tell him what he wants to know, Toby," Renada said. Mallon narrowed his eyes at her. "You'll live to regret this, Renada."

"Maybe I will, Toby. But you taught me how to handle a gun—and to play cards for keeps."

The flush faded out of his face and left it pale. "All right, Jackson," he said, almost in a whisper. "It's not only the equipment. It's... the men."

I heard a clock ticking somewhere.

"What men, Toby?" I said softly.

"The crew. Day, Macy, the others. They're still in there, Jackson—aboard the ship, in stasis. We were trying to get the ship off when the attack came. There was forty minutes' warning. Everything was ready to go. You were on a test run; there wasn't time to cycle you out ...."

"Keep talking," I rapped.

"You know how the system was set up; it was to be a ten-year run out, with an automatic turnaround at the end of that time if Alpha Centauri wasn't within a milliparsec." He snorted. "It wasn't. After twenty years, the instruments checked. They were satisfied. There was a planetary mass within the acceptable range. So they brought me out." He snorted again. "The longest dry run in history. I unstrapped and came out to see what was going on. It took me a little while to realize what had happened. I went back in and cycled Banner and

Mackenzie out. We went into the town; you know what we found. I saw what we had to do, but Banner and Mac argued. The fools wanted to reseal *Prometheus* and proceed with the launch. For what? So we could spend the rest of our lives squatting in the ruins, when by stripping the ship we could make ourselves kings?"

"So there was an argument?" I prompted.

"I had a gun. I hit Mackenzie in the leg, I think—but they got clear, found a car and beat me to the Site. There were two Bolos. What chance did I have against them?" Mallon grinned craftily. "But Banner was a fool. He died for it." The grin dropped like a stripper's bra. "But when I went to claim my spoils, I discovered how the jackals had set the trap for me."

"That was downright unfriendly of them, Mallon. Oddly enough, it doesn't make me want to stay and hold your hand."

"Don't you understand yet!" Mallon's voice was a dry screech. "Even if you got clear of the palace, used the Bolo to set yourself up as Baron—you'd never be safe! Not as long as one man was still alive aboard the ship. You'd never have a night's rest, wondering when one of them would walk out to challenge your rule …."

"Uneasy lies the head, eh, Toby? You remind me of a queen bee. The first one out of the chrysalis dismembers all her rivals."

"I don't mean to kill them. That would be a waste; I mean to give them useful work to do."

"I don't think they'd like being your slaves, Toby. And neither would I." I looked at Renada. "I'll be leaving you now," I said. "Whichever way you decide, good luck."

"Wait." She stood. "I'm going with you."

I looked at her. "I'll be traveling fast, honey. And that gun in my back may throw off my timing."

She stepped to me, reversed the pistol, and laid it in my hand.

"Don't kill him, Mr. Jackson. He was always kind to me."

"Why change sides now? According to Toby, my chances look not too good."

"I never knew before how Commander Banner died," she said. "He was my great-grandfather."

7

Renada came back bundled in a gray fur as I finished buckling on my holster.

"So long, Toby," I said. "I ought to shoot you in the belly just for Don, but—"

I saw Renada's eyes widen at the same instant that I heard the click.

I dropped flat and rolled behind Mallon's chair—and a gout of blue flame yammered into the spot where I'd been standing. I whipped the gun up and fired a round into the peach-colored upholstery an inch from Toby's ear.

"The next one nails you to the chair," I yelled. "Call 'em off!" There was a moment of dead silence. Toby sat frozen. I couldn't see who'd been doing the shooting. Then I heard a moan. Renada.

"Let the girl alone or I'll kill him," I called.

Toby sat rigid, his eyes rolled toward me.

"You can't kill me, Jackson! I'm all that's keeping you alive."

"You can't kill me either, Toby. You need my magic touch, remember? Maybe you'd better give me a safe-conduct out of here. I'll take the freeze off your Bolo—after I've seen to my business."

Toby licked his lips. I heard Renada again. She was trying not to moan—but moaning anyway. "You tried, Jackson. It didn't work out," Toby said through gritted teeth. "Throw out your gun and stand up. I won't kill you—you know that. You do as you're told and you may still live to a ripe old age—and the girl, too."

She screamed then—a mindless ululation of pure agony.

"Hurry up, you fool, before they tear her arm off," Mallon grated. "Or shoot. You'll get to watch her for twenty-four hours under the knife. Then you'll have your turn."

I fired again—closer this time. Mallon jerked his head and cursed.

"If they touch her again, you get it, Toby," I said. "Send her over here. Move!"

"Let her go!" Mallon snarled. Renada stumbled into sight, moved around the chair, then crumpled suddenly to the rug beside me.

"Stand up, Toby," I ordered. He rose slowly. Sweat glistened on his face now. "Stand over here." He moved like a sleepwalker. I got to my feet. There were two men standing across the room beside a small open door. A sliding panel. Both of them held power rifles leveled— but aimed offside, away from the Baron.

"Drop 'em!" I said. They looked at me, then lowered the guns, tossed them aside.

I opened my mouth to tell Mallon to move ahead, but my tongue felt thick and heavy. The room was suddenly full of smoke. In front of me, Mallon was wavering like a mirage. I started to tell him to stand still, but with my thick tongue, it was too much trouble. I raised the gun, but somehow it was falling to the floor—slowly, like a leaf—and then I was floating, too, on waves that broke on a dark sea ....

"Do you think you're the first idiot who thought he could kill me?" Mallon raised a contemptuous lip. "This room's rigged ten different ways."

I shook my head, trying to ignore the film before my eyes and the nausea in my body. "No, I imagine lots of people would like a crack at you, Toby. One day one of them's going to make it."

"Get him on his feet," Mallon snapped. Hard hands clamped on my arms, hauled me off the cot. I worked my legs, but they were like yesterday's celery; I sagged against somebody who smelled like uncured hides.

"You seem drowsy," Mallon said. "We'll see if we can't wake you up."

A thumb dug into my neck. I jerked away, and a jab under the ribs doubled me over.

"I have to keep you alive—for the moment," Mallon said. "But you won't get a lot of pleasure out of it."

I blinked hard. It was dark in the room. One of my handlers had a ring of beard around his mouth—I could see that much. Mallon was standing before me, hands on hips. I aimed a kick at him, just for fun. It didn't work out; my foot seemed to be wearing a lead boat. The unshaven man hit me in the mouth and Toby chuckled.

"Have your fun, Dunger," he said, "but I'll want him alive and on his feet for the night's work. Take him out and walk him in the fresh air. Report to me at the Pavilion of the Troll in an hour." He turned to something and gave orders about lights and gun emplacements, and I heard Renada's name mentioned.

Then he was gone and I was being dragged through the door and along the corridor.

The exercise helped. By the time the hour had passed, I was feeling weak but normal—except for an aching head and a feeling that there was a strand of spiderweb interfering with my vision. Toby had given me a good meal. Maybe before the night was over he'd regret that mistake ....

Across the dark grounds, an engine started up, spluttered, then settled down to a steady hum.

"It's time," the one with the whiskers said. He had a voice like soft cheese to match his smell. He took another half-twist in the arm he was holding.

"Don't break it," I grunted. "It belongs to the Baron, remember?"

Whiskers stopped dead. "You talk too much—and too smart." He let my arm go and stepped back. "Hold him, Pig Eye." The other man whipped a forearm across my throat and levered my head back; then Whiskers unlimbered the two-foot club from his belt and hit me hard in the side, just under the ribs. Pig Eye let go and I folded over and waited while the pain swelled up and burst inside me.

Then they hauled me back to my feet. I couldn't feel any bone ends grating, so there probably weren't any broken ribs—if that was any consolation.

There were lights glaring now across the lawn. Moving figures cast long shadows against the trees lining the drive—and on the side of the Bolo Combat Unit parked under its canopy by the sealed gate.

A crude breastwork had been thrown up just over fifty yards from it. A wheel-mounted generator putted noisily in the background, laying a layer of bluish exhaust in the air.

Mallon was waiting with a 9-mm power rifle in his hands as we came up, my two guards gripping me with both hands to demonstrate their zeal, and me staggering a little more than was necessary. I saw Renada standing by, wrapped in a gray fur. Her face looked white in the harsh light. She made a move toward me and a greenback caught her arm.

"You know what to do, Jackson," Mallon said speaking loudly against the clatter of the generator. He made a curt gesture and a man stepped up and buckled a stout chain to my left ankle. Mallon held out my electropass. "I want you to walk straight to the Bolo. Go in by the side port. You've got one minute to cancel the instructions punched into the command circuit and climb back outside. If you don't show, I close a switch there—" He pointed to a wooden box mounting an open circuit-breaker, with a tangle of heavy cable leading toward the Bolo—"and you cook in your shoes. The same thing happens if I see the guns start to traverse or the antipersonnel ports open." I followed the coils of armored wire from the chain on my ankle back to the wooden box—and on to the generator.

"Crude, maybe, but it will work. And if you get any idea of letting fly a round or two at random—remember the girl will be right beside me."

I looked across at the giant machine. "Suppose it doesn't recognize me? It's been a while. Or what if Don didn't plug my identity pattern in to the recognition circuit?"

"In that case, you're no good to me anyway," Mallon said flatly.

I caught Renada's eye, gave her a wink and a smile I didn't feel, and climbed up on top of the revetment.

I looked back at Mallon. He was old and shrunken in the garish light, his smooth gray suit rumpled, his thin hair mussed, the gun held in a white-knuckled grip. He looked more like a harassed shopkeeper than a would-be world-beater.

"You must want the Bolo pretty bad to take the chance, Toby," I said. "I'll think about taking that wild shot. You sweat me out."

I flipped slack into the wire trailing my ankle, jumped down, and started across the smooth-trimmed grass, a long black shadow stalking before me. The Bolo sat silent, as big as a bank in the circle of the spotlight. I could see the flecks of rust now around the port covers, the small vines that twined up her sides from the ragged stands of weeds that marked no-man's-land.

There was something white in the brush ahead. Broken human bones.

I felt my stomach go rigid again. The last man had gotten this far; I wasn't in the clear yet ….

I passed two more scattered skeletons in the next twenty feet. They must have come in on the run, guinea pigs to test the alertness of the Bolo. Or maybe they'd tried creeping up, dead slow, an inch a day; it hadn't worked ….

Tiny night creatures scuttled ahead. They would be safe here in the shadow of the troll where no predator bigger than a mouse could move. I stumbled, diverted my course around a ten-foot hollow, the eroded crater of a near miss.

Now I could see the great moss-coated treads sunk a foot into the earth, the nests of field mice tucked in the spokes of the yard-high bogies. The entry hatch was above, a hairline against the great curved flank. There were rungs set in the flaring tread shield. I reached up, got a grip and hauled myself up. My chain clanked against the metal. I found the door lever, held on and pulled.

It resisted, then turned. There was the hum of a servo motor, a crackling of dead gaskets. The hairline widened and showed me a narrow companionway, green-anodized dural with black polymer treads, a bulkhead with a fire extinguisher, an embossed steel data plate that said BOLO DIVISION OF GENERAL MOTORS CORPORATION and below, in smaller type, UNIT, COMBAT, BOLO MARK III.

I pulled myself inside and went up into the Christmas-tree glow of instrument lights.

The control cockpit was small, utilitarian, with two deep-padded seats set among screens, dials, levers. I sniffed the odors of oil, paint, the characteristic ether and ozone of a nuclear generator. There was a faint hum in the air from idling relay servos. The clock showed ten past four. Either it was later than I thought, or the chronometer had lost time in the last eighty years. But I had no time to lose ....

I slid into the seat, flipped back the cover of the command control console. The Cancel key was the big white one. I pulled it down and let it snap back, like a clerk ringing up a sale.

A pattern of dots on the status-display screen flicked out of existence. Mallon was safe from his pet troll now.

It hadn't taken me long to carry out my orders. I knew what to do next; I'd planned it all during my walk out. Now I had thirty seconds to stack the deck in my favor.

I reached down, hauled the festoon of quarter-inch armored cable up in front of me. I hit a switch, and the inner conning cover—a disk of inch-thick armor—slid back. I shoved a loop of the flexible cable up through the aperture, reversed the switch. The cover slid back—slicing the armored cable like macaroni.

I took a deep breath, and my hands went to the combat alert switch, hovered over it.

It was the smart thing to do—the easy thing. All I had to do was punch a key, and the 9-mm's would open up, scythe Mallon and his crew down like cornstalks.

But the scything would mow Renada down, along with the rest. And if I went—even without firing a shot—Mallon would keep his promise to cut that white throat ….

My head was out of the noose now, but I would have to put it back—for a while.

I leaned sideways, reached back under the panel, groped for a small fuse box. My fingers were clumsy. I took a breath, tried again. The fuse dropped out in my hand. The Bolo's I-R circuit was dead now. With a few more seconds to work, I could have knocked out other circuits—but the time had run out.

I grabbed the cut ends of my lead wire, knotted them around the chain and got out fast.

8

Mallon waited, crouched behind the revetment.

"It's safe now, is it?" he grated. I nodded. He stood, gripping his gun. "Now we'll try it together."

I went over the parapet, Mallon following with his gun ready. The lights followed us to the Bolo. Mallon clambered up to the open port, looked around inside, then dropped back down beside me. He looked excited now.

"That does it, Jackson! I've waited a long time for this. Now I've got all the *mana* there is!"

"Take a look at the cable on my ankle," I said softly. He narrowed his eyes, stepped back, gun aimed, darted a glance at the cable looped to the chain.

"I cut it, Toby. I was alone in the Bolo with the cable cut—and I didn't fire. I could have taken your toy and set up in business for myself, but I didn't."

"What's that supposed to buy you?" Mallon rasped.

"As you said—we need each other. That cut cable proves you can trust me."

Mallon smiled. It wasn't a nice smile. "Safe, were you? Come here." I walked along with him to the back of the Bolo. A heavy copper wire hung across the rear of the machine, trailing off into the grass in both directions.

"I'd have burned you at the first move. Even with the cable cut, the armored cover would have carried the full load right into the cockpit with you. But don't be nervous. I've got other jobs for you." He jabbed the gun muzzle hard into my chest, pushing me back. "Now get moving," he snarled. "And don't ever threaten the Baron again."

"The years have done more than shrivel your face, Toby," I said. "They've cracked your brain."

He laughed, a short bark. "You could be right. What's sane and what isn't? I've got a vision in my mind—and I'll make it come true. If that's insanity, it's better than what the mob has."

Back at the parapet, Mallon turned to me. "I've had this campaign planned in detail for years, Jackson. Everything's ready. We move out in half an hour—before any traitors have time to take word to my enemies. Pig Eye and Dunger will keep you from being lonely while I'm away. When I get back—Well, maybe you're right about working together." He gestured and my whiskery friend and his sidekick loomed up. "Watch him," he said.

"Genghis Khan is on the march, eh?" I said, "With nothing between you and the goodies but a five-hundred-ton Bolo ...."

"The Lesser Troll ...." He raised his hands and made crushing motions, like a man crumbling dry earth. "I'll trample it under my treads."

"You're confused, Toby. The Bolo has treads. You just have a couple of fallen arches."

"It's the same. I am the Great Troll." He showed me his teeth and walked away.

I moved along between Dunger and Pig Eye, toward the lights of the garage.

"The back entrance again," I said. "Anyone would think you were ashamed of me."

"You need more training, hah?" Dunger rasped. "Hold him, Pig Eye." He unhooked his club and swung it loosely in his hand, glancing around. We were near the trees by the drive. There was no one in sight except the crews near the Bolo and a group by the front of the palace. Pig Eye gave my arm a twist and shifted his grip to his old favorite strangle hold. I was hoping he would.

Dunger whipped the club up, and I grabbed Pig Eye's arm with both hands and leaned forward like a Japanese admiral reporting to the Emperor. Pig Eye went up and over just in time to catch Dunger's club across the back. They went down together. I went for the club, but Whiskers was faster than he looked. He rolled clear, got to his knees, and laid it across my left arm, just below the shoulder.

I heard the bone go ....

I was back on my feet, somehow. Pig Eye lay sprawled before me. I heard him whining as though from a great distance. Dunger stood six feet away, the ring of black beard spread in a grin like a hyena smelling dead meat.

"His back's broke," he said. "Hell of a sound he's making. I been waiting for you; I wanted you to hear it."

"I've heard it," I managed. My voice seemed to be coming off a worn soundtrack. "Surprised ... you didn't work me over ... while I was busy with the arm."

"Uh-uh. I like a man to know what's going on when I work him over." He stepped in, rapped the broken arm lightly with the club. Fiery agony choked a groan off in my throat. I backed a step; he stalked me.

"Pig Eye wasn't much, but he was my pal. When I'm through with you, I'll have to kill him. A man with a broken back's no use to nobody. His'll be finished pretty soon now, but not with you. You'll be around a long time yet; but I'll get a lot of fun out of you before the Baron gets back."

I was under the trees now. I had some wild thoughts about grabbing up a club of my own, but they were just thoughts. Dunger set himself and his eyes dropped to my belly. I didn't wait for it; I lunged at him. He laughed and stepped back, and the club cracked my head.

Not hard; just enough to send me down. I got my legs under me and started to get up—

There was a hint of motion from the shadows behind Dunger. I shook my head to cover any expression that might have showed, let myself drop back.

"Get up," Dunger said. The smile was gone now. He aimed a kick. "Get up—"

He froze suddenly, then whirled. His hearing must have been as keen as a jungle cat's; I hadn't heard a sound.

The old man stepped into view, his white hair plastered wet to his skull, his big hands spread. Dunger snarled, jumped in and whipped the club down; I heard it hit. There was a flurry of struggle, then Dunger stumbled back, empty-handed.

I was on my feet again now. I made a lunge for Dunger as he roared and charged. The club in the old man's hand rose and fell. Dunger crashed past and into the brush. The old man sat down suddenly, still holding the club. Then he let it fall and lay back. I went toward him and Dunger rushed me from the side. I went down again.

I was dazed, but not feeling any pain now. Dunger was standing over the old man. I could see the big lean figure lying limply, arms outspread—and a white bone handle, incongruously new and neat against the shabby mackinaw. The club lay on the ground a few feet away. I started crawling for it. It seemed a long way, and it was hard for me to move my legs, but I kept at it. The light rain was falling again now, hardly more than a mist. Far away there were shouts and the sound of engines starting up. Mallon's convoy moving out. He had won. Dunger had won, too. The old man had tried, but it hadn't been enough. But if I could reach the club, and swing it just once ....

Dunger was looking down at the old man. He leaned, withdrew the knife, wiped it on his trouser leg, hitching up his pants to tuck it away in its sheath. The club was smooth and heavy under my hand. I got a good grip on it, got to my feet. I waited until Dunger turned, and then I hit him across the top of the skull with everything I had left ....

I thought the old man was dead until he blinked suddenly. His features looked relaxed now, peaceful, the skin like parchment stretched over bone. I took his gnarled old hand and rubbed it. It was as cold as a drowned sailor.

"You waited for me, old timer?" I said inanely. He moved his head minutely, and looked at me. Then his mouth moved. I leaned close to catch what he was saying. His voice was fainter than lost hope.

"Mom ... told ... me ... wait for you .... She said ... you'd ... come back some day ...."

I felt my jaw muscles knotting.

Inside me something broke and flowed away like molten metal. Suddenly my eyes were blurred—and not only with rain. I looked at the old face before me, and for a moment, I seemed to see a ghostly glimpse of another face, a small round face that looked up.

He was speaking again. I put my head down:

"Was I ... good ... boy ... Dad?" Then the eyes closed.

I sat for a long time, looking at the still face. Then I folded the hands on the chest and stood.

"You were more than a good boy, Timmy," I said. "You were a good man."

9

My blue suit was soaking wet and splattered with mud, plus a few flecks of what Dunger had used for brains, but it still carried the gold eagles on the shoulders.

The attendant in the garage didn't look at my face. The eagles were enough for him. I stalked to a vast black Bentley—a '90 model, I guessed, from the conservative eighteen-inch tail fins—and jerked the door open. The gauge showed three-quarters full. I opened the glove compartment, rummaged, found nothing. But then it wouldn't be up front with the chauffeur ....

I pulled open the back door. There was a crude black leather holster riveted against the smooth pale-gray leather, with the butt of a 4-mm showing. There was another one on the opposite door, and a power rifle slung from straps on the back of the driver's seat.

Whoever owned the Bentley was overcompensating his insecurity. I took a pistol, tossed it onto the front seat, and slid in beside it. The attendant gaped at me as I eased my left arm into my lap and twisted to close the door. I started up. There was a bad knock, but she ran all right. I flipped a switch and cold lances of light speared out into the rain.

At the last instant, the attendant started forward with his mouth open to say something, but I didn't wait to hear it. I gunned out into the night, swung into the graveled drive, and headed for the gate. Mallon had had it all his way so far, but maybe it still wasn't too late ....

Two sentries, looking miserable in shiny black ponchos, stepped out of the guard hut as I pulled up. One peered in at me, then came to a sloppy position of attention and presented arms. I reached for the gas pedal and the second sentry called something. The first man looked startled, then swung the gun down to cover me. I eased a hand toward my pistol, brought it up fast, and fired through the glass. Then the Bentley was roaring off into the dark along the pot-holed road that led into town. I thought I heard a shot behind me, but I wasn't sure.

I took the river road south of town, pounding at reckless speed over the ruined blacktop, gaining on the lights of Mallon's horde paralleling me a mile to the north. A quarter mile from the perimeter fence, the Bentley broke a spring and skidded into a ditch.

I sat for a moment taking deep breaths to drive back the compulsive drowsiness that was sliding down over my eyes like a visor. My arm throbbed like a cauterized stump. I needed a few minutes' rest ....

A sound brought me awake like an old maid smelling cigar smoke in the bedroom: the rise and fall of heavy engines in convoy. Mallon was coming up at flank speed.

I got out of the car and headed off along the road at a trot, holding my broken arm with my good one to ease the jarring pain. My chances had been as slim as a gambler's wallet all along, but if Mallon beat me to the objective, they dropped to nothing.

The eastern sky had taken on a faint gray tinge, against which I could make out the silhouetted gateposts and the dead floodlights a hundred yards ahead.

The roar of engines was getting louder. There were other sounds, too: a few shouts, the chatter of a 9-mm, the *boom!* of something heavier, and once a long-drawn *whoosh!* of falling masonry. With his new toy, Mallon was dozing his way through the men and buildings that got in his way.

I reached the gate, picked my way over fallen wire mesh, then headed for the Primary Site.

I couldn't run now. The broken slabs tilted crazily, in no pattern. I slipped, stumbled, but kept my feet. Behind me, headlights threw shadows across the slabs. It wouldn't be long now before someone in Mallon's task force spotted me and opened up with the guns—

The whoop! *whoop!* WHOOP! of the guardian Bolo cut across the field.

Across the broken concrete I saw the two red eyes flash, sweeping my way. I looked toward the gate. A massed rank of vehicles stood in a battalion front just beyond the old perimeter fence, engines idling, ranged for a hundred yards on either side of a wide gap at the gate. I looked for the high silhouette of Mallon's Bolo, and saw it far off down the avenue, picked out in red, white, and green navigation lights, a jeweled dreadnought. A glaring Cyclopean eye at the top darted a blue-white cone of light ahead, swept over the waiting escort, outlined me like a set-shifter caught onstage by the rising curtain.

The *whoop! whoop!* sounded again; the automated sentry Bolo was bearing down on me along the dancing lane of light.

I grabbed at the plastic disk in my pocket as though holding it in my hand would somehow heighten its potency. I didn't know if the Lesser Troll was programmed to exempt me from destruction or not; and there was only one way to find out.

It wasn't too late to turn around and run for it. Mallon might shoot—or he might not. I could convince him that he needed me, that together we could grab twice as much loot. And then, when he died—

I wasn't really considering it; it was the kind of thought that flashes through a man's mind like heat lightning when time slows in the instant of crisis. It was hard to be brave with broken bone ends grating, but what I had to do didn't take courage. I was a small, soft, human grub, stepped on but still moving, caught on the harsh plain of broken concrete between the clash of chrome-steel titans. But I knew which direction to take.

The Lesser Troll rushed toward me in a roll of thunder and I went to meet it.

It stopped twenty yards from me, loomed massive as a cliff. Its heavy guns were dead, I knew. Without them it was no more dangerous than a farmer with a shotgun—

But against me a shotgun was enough.

The slab under me trembled as if in anticipation. I squinted against the dull red I-R beams that pivoted to hold me, waiting while the Troll considered. Then the guns elevated, pointed over my head like a benediction. The Bolo knew me.

The guns traversed fractionally. I looked back toward the enemy line, saw the Great Troll coming up now, closing the gap, towering over its waiting escort like a planet among moons. And the guns of the Lesser Troll tracked it as it came—the empty guns that for twenty years had held Mallon's scavengers at bay.

The noise of engines was deafening now. The waiting line moved restlessly, pulverizing old concrete under churning treads. I didn't realize I was being fired on until I saw chips fly to my left and heard the howl of ricochets.

It was time to move. I scrambled for the Bolo, snorted at the stink of hot oil and ozone, found the rusted handholds, and pulled myself up—

Bullets spanged off metal above me. Someone was trying for me with a power rifle.

The broken arm hung at my side like a fence post nailed to my shoulder, but I wasn't aware of the pain now. The hatch stood open half an inch. I grabbed the lever, strained; it swung wide. No lights came up to meet me. With the port cracked, they'd burned out long ago. I dropped down inside, wriggled through the narrow crawl space into the cockpit. It was smaller than the Mark III—and it was occupied.

In the faint green light from the panel, the dead man crouched over the controls, one desiccated hand in a shriveled black glove clutching the control bar. He wore a GI weather suit and a white crash helmet, and one foot was twisted nearly backward, caught behind a jack lever.

The leg had been broken before he died. He must have jammed the foot and twisted it so that the pain would hold off the sleep that had come at last. I leaned forward to see the face. The blackened and mummified features showed only the familiar anonymity of death, but the bushy reddish mustache was enough.

"Hello, Mac," I said. "Sorry to keep you waiting; I got held up."

I wedged myself into the copilot's seat, flipped the I-R screen switch. The eight-inch panel glowed, showed me the enemy Bolo trampling through the fence three hundred yards away, then moving onto the ramp, dragging a length of rusty chain-link like a bridal train behind it.

I put my hand on the control bar. "I'll take it now, Mac." I moved the bar, and the dead man's hand moved with it.

"Okay, Mac," I said. "We'll do it together."

I hit the switches, canceling the preset response pattern. It had done its job for eighty years, but now it was time to crank in a little human strategy.

My Bolo rocked slightly under a hit and I heard the tread shields drop down. The chair bucked under me as Mallon moved in, pouring in the fire.

Beside me Mac nodded patiently. It was old stuff to him. I watched the tracers on the screen. Hosing me down with contact exploders probably gave Mallon a lot of satisfaction, but it couldn't hurt me. It would be a different story when he tired of the game and tried the heavy stuff.

I threw in the drive, backed rapidly. Mallon's tracers followed for a few yards, then cut off abruptly. I pivoted, flipped on my polyarcs, raced for the position I had selected across the field, then swung to face Mallon as he moved toward me. It had been a long time since he had handled the controls of a Bolo; he was rusty, relying on his automatics. I had no heavy rifles, but my popguns were okay. I homed my 4-mm solid-slug cannon on Mallon's polyarc, pressed the FIRE button.

There was a scream from the high-velocity-feed magazine. The blue-white light flared and went out. The Bolo's defense could handle anything short of an H-bomb, pick a missile out of the stratosphere fifty miles away, devastate a county with one round from its mortars—but my BB gun at point-blank range had poked out its eye.

I switched everything off and sat silent, waiting. Mallon had come to a dead stop. I could picture him staring at the dark screens, slapping levers, and cursing. He would be confused, wondering what had happened. With his lights gone, he'd be on radar now—not very sensitive at this range, not too conscious of detail ....

I watched my panel. An amber warning light winked. Mallon's radar was locked on me.

He moved forward again, then stopped; he was having trouble making up his mind. I flipped a key to drop a padded shock frame in place and braced myself. Mallon would be getting mad now.

Crimson danger lights flared on the board and I rocked under the recoil as my interceptors flashed out to meet Mallon's C-S C's and detonate them in incandescent rendezvous over the scarred concrete between us. My screens went white, then dropped back to secondary brilliance, flashing stark black-and-white. My ears hummed like trapped hornets.

The sudden silence was like a vault door closing.

I sagged back, feeling like Quasimodo after a wild ride on the bells. The screens blinked bright again, and I watched Mallon, sitting motionless now in his near blindness. On his radar screen I would show as a blurred hill; he would be wondering why I hadn't returned his fire, why I hadn't turned and run, why ... why ....

He lurched and started toward me. I waited, then eased back, slowly. He accelerated, closing in to come to grips at a range where even the split microsecond response of my defenses would be too slow to hold off his fire. And I backed, letting him gain, but not too fast ....

Mallon couldn't wait.

He opened up, throwing a mixed bombardment from his 9-mm's, his infinite repeaters, and his C-S C's. I held on, fighting the battering frame, watching the screens. The gap closed; a hundred yards, ninety, eighty.

The open silo yawned in Mallon's path now, but he didn't see it. The mighty Bolo came on, guns bellowing in the night, closing for the kill. On the brink of the fifty-foot-wide, hundred-yard-deep pit, it hesitated as though sensing danger. Then it moved forward.

I saw it rock, dropping its titanic prow, showing its broad back, gouging the blasted pavement as its guns bore on the ground. Great sheets of sparks flew as the treads reversed, too late. The Bolo hung for a moment longer, then slid down majestically as a sinking liner, its guns still firing into the pit like a challenge to Hell. And then it was gone. A dust cloud boiled for a moment, then whipped away as displaced air tornadoed from the open mouth of the silo.

And the earth trembled under the impact far below.

10

The doors of the Primary Site blockhouse were nine-foot-high, eight-inch-thick panels of solid chromalloy that even a Bolo would have slowed down for, but they slid aside for my electropass like a shower curtain at the YW. I went into a shadowy room where eighty years of silence hung like black crepe on a coffin. The tiled floor was still immaculate, the air fresh. Here at the heart of the Aerospace Center, all systems were still go.

In the Central Control bunker, nine rows of green lights glowed on the high panel over red letters that spelled out STAND BY TO FIRE. A foot to the left, the big white lever stood in the unlocked position, six inches from the outstretched fingertips of the mummified corpse strapped into the controller's chair. To the right, a red glow on the monitor panel indicated the lock doors open.

I rode the lift down to K level, stepped out onto the steel-railed platform that hugged the sweep of the starship's hull and stepped through into the narrow COC.

On my right, three empty stasis tanks stood open, festooned cabling draped in disorder. To the left were the four sealed covers under which Day, Macy, Cruciani, and Black waited. I went close, read dials. Slender needles trembled minutely to the beating of sluggish hearts.

They were alive.

I left the ship, sealed the inner and outer ports. Back in the control bunker, the monitor panel showed ALL CLEAR FOR LAUNCH now. I studied the timer, set it, turned back to the master panel. The white lever was smooth and cool under my hand. It seated with a click. The red hand of the launch clock moved off jerkily, the ticking harsh in the silence.

Outside, the Bolo waited. I climbed to a perch in the open conning tower twenty feet above the broken pavement, moved off toward the west where sunrise colors picked out the high towers of the palace.

I rested the weight of my splinted and wrapped arm on the balcony rail, looking out across the valley and the town to the misty plain under which *Prometheus* waited.

"There's something happening now," Renada said. I took the binoculars, watched as the silo doors rolled back.

"There's smoke," Renada said.

"Don't worry, just cooling gases being vented off." I looked at my watch. "Another minute or two and man makes the biggest jump since the first lungfish crawled out on a mud flat."

"What will they find out there?"

I shook my head. "*Homo terra firma* can't even conceive of what *Homo astra* has ahead of him."

"Twenty years they'll be gone. It's a long time to wait."

"We'll be busy trying to put together a world for them to come back to. I don't think we'll be bored."

"Look!" Renada gripped my good arm. A long silvery shape, huge even at the distance of miles, rose slowly out of the earth, poised on a brilliant ball of white fire. Then the sound came, a thunder that penetrated my bones, shook the railing under my hand. The fireball lengthened into a silver-white column with the ship balanced at its tip. Then the column broke free, rose up, up ....

I felt Renada's hand touch mine. I gripped it hard. Together we watched as *Prometheus* took man's gift of fire back to the heavens.

Courier

"It is rather unusual," Magnan said, "to assign an officer of your rank to courier duty, but this is an unusual mission."

Retief sat relaxed and said nothing. Just before the silence grew awkward, Magnan went on.

"There are four planets in the group," he said. "Two double planets, all rather close to an unimportant star listed as DRI-G 33987. They're called Jorgensen's Worlds, and in themselves are of no importance whatever. However, they lie deep in the sector into which the Soetti have been penetrating.

"Now—" Magnan leaned forward and lowered his voice—"we have learned that the Soetti plan a bold step forward. Since they've met no opposition so far in their infiltration of Terrestrial space, they intend to seize Jorgensen's Worlds by force."

Magnan leaned back, waiting for Retief's reaction. Retief drew carefully on his cigar and looked at Magnan. Magnan frowned.

"This is open aggression, Retief," he said, "in case I haven't made myself clear. Aggression on Terrestrial-occupied territory by an alien species. Obviously, we can't allow it."

Magnan drew a large folder from his desk.

"A show of resistance at this point is necessary. Unfortunately, Jorgensen's Worlds are technologically undeveloped areas. They're farmers or traders. Their industry is limited to a minor role in their economy—enough to support the merchant fleet, no more. The war potential, by conventional standards, is nil."

Magnan tapped the folder before him.

"I have here," he said solemnly, "information which will change that picture completely." He leaned back and blinked at Retief.

"All right, Mr. Counselor," Retief said. "I'll play along; what's in the folder?"

Magnan spread his fingers, folded one down.

"First," he said. "The Soetti War Plan—in detail. We were fortunate enough to make contact with a defector from a party of renegade Terrestrials who've been advising the Soetti." He folded another finger. "Next, a battle plan for the Jorgensen's people, worked out by the Theory group." He wrestled a third finger down. "Lastly, an Utter Top Secret schematic for conversion of a standard antiacceleration field into a potent weapon—a development our systems people have been holding in reserve for just such a situation."

"Is that all?" Retief said. "You've still got two fingers sticking up."

Magnan looked at the fingers and put them away.

"This is no occasion for flippancy, Retief. In the wrong hands, this information could be catastrophic. You'll memorize it before you leave this building."

"I'll carry it, sealed," Retief said. "That way nobody can sweat it out of me."

Magnan started to shake his head.

"Well," he said. "If it's trapped for destruction, I suppose—"

"I've heard of these Jorgensen's Worlds," Retief said. "I remember an agent, a big blond fellow, very quick on the uptake. A wizard with cards and dice. Never played for money, though."

"Umm," Magnan said. "Don't make the error of personalizing this situation, Retief. Overall policy calls for a defense of these backwater worlds. Otherwise the Corps would allow history to follow its natural course, as always."

"When does this attack happen?"

"Less than four weeks."

"That doesn't leave me much time."

"I have your itinerary here. Your accommodations are clear as far as Aldo Cerise. You'll have to rely on your ingenuity to get you the rest of the way."

"That's a pretty rough trip, Mr. Counselor. Suppose I don't make it?"

Magnan looked sour. "Someone at a policy-making level has chosen to put all our eggs in one basket, Retief. I hope their confidence in you is not misplaced."

"This antiac conversion; how long does it take?"

"A skilled electronics crew can do the job in a matter of minutes. The Jorgensens can handle it very nicely; every other man is a mechanic of some sort."

Retief opened the envelope Magnan handed him and looked at the tickets inside.

"Less than four hours to departure time," he said. "I'd better not start any long books."

"You'd better waste no time getting over to Indoctrination," Magnan said.

Retief stood up. "If I hurry, maybe I can catch the cartoon."

"The allusion escapes me," Magnan said coldly. "And one last word. The Soetti are patrolling the trade lanes into Jorgensen's Worlds; don't get yourself interned."

"I'll tell you what," Retief said soberly. "In a pinch, I'll mention your name."

"You'll be traveling with Class X credentials," Magnan snapped. "There must be nothing to connect you with the Corps."

"They'll never guess," Retief said. "I'll pose as a gentleman."

"You'd better be getting started," Magnan said, shuffling papers.

"You're right," Retief said. "If I work at it, I might manage a snootful by takeoff." He went to the door. "No objection to my checking out a needler, is there?"

Magnan looked up. "I suppose not. What do you want with it?"

"Just a feeling I've got."

"Please yourself."

"Some day," Retief said, "I may take you up on that."

2

Retief put down the heavy travel-battered suitcase and leaned on the counter, studying the schedules chalked on the board under the legend "ALDO CERISE—INTERPLANETARY." A thin clerk in a faded sequined blouse and a plastic snakeskin cummerbund groomed his fingernails, watching Retief from the corner of his eye.

Retief glanced at him.

The clerk nipped off a ragged corner with rabbitlike front teeth and spat it on the floor.

"Was there something?" he said.

"Two twenty-eight, due out today for the Jorgensen group," Retief said. "Is it on schedule?"

The clerk sampled the inside of his right cheek, eyed Retief. "Filled up. Try again in a couple of weeks."

"What time does it leave?"

"I don't think—"

"Let's stick to facts," Retief said. "Don't try to think. What time is it due out?"

The clerk smiled pityingly. "It's my lunch hour," he said. "I'll be open in an hour." He held up a thumbnail, frowned at it.

"If I have to come around this counter," Retief said, "I'll feed that thumb to you the hard way."

The clerk looked up and opened his mouth. Then he caught Retief's eye, closed his mouth and swallowed.

"Like it says there," he said, jerking a thumb at the board. "Lifts in an hour. But you won't be on it," he added.

Retief looked at him.

"Some … ah … VIP's required accommodation," he said. He hooked a finger inside the sequined collar. "All tourist reservations were canceled. You'll have to try to get space on the Four-Planet Line ship next—"

"Which gate?" Retief said.

"For … ah …?"

"For two twenty-eight for Jorgensen's Worlds," Retief said.

"Well," the clerk said. "Gate nineteen," he added quickly. "But—"

Retief picked up his suitcase and walked away toward the glare sign reading *To Gates 16–30.*

"Another smart aleck," the clerk said behind him.

Retief followed the signs, threaded his way through crowds, found a covered ramp with the number 228 posted over it. A heavy-shouldered man with a scarred jawline and small eyes was slouching there in a rumpled gray uniform. He put out a hand as Retief started past him.

"Lessee your boarding pass," he muttered.

Retief pulled a paper from an inside pocket, handed it over.

The guard blinked at it.

"Whassat?"

"A gram confirming my space," Retief said. "Your boy on the counter says he's out to lunch."

The guard crumpled the gram, dropped it on the floor and lounged back against the handrail.

"On your way, bub," he said.

Retief put his suitcase carefully on the floor, took a step, and drove a right into the guard's midriff. He stepped aside as the man doubled and went to his knees.

"You were wide open, ugly. I couldn't resist. Tell your boss I sneaked past while you were resting your eyes." He picked up his bag, stepped over the man, and went up the gangway into the ship.

A cabin boy in stained whites came along the corridor.

"Which way to cabin fifty-seven, son?" Retief asked.

"Up there." The boy jerked his head and hurried on. Retief made his way along the narrow hall, found signs, followed them to cabin fifty-seven. The door was open. Inside, baggage was piled in the center of the floor. It was expensive-looking baggage.

Retief put his bag down. He turned at a sound behind him. A tall, florid man with an expensive coat belted over a massive paunch stood in the open door, looking at Retief. Retief looked back. The florid man clamped his jaws together, turned to speak over his shoulder.

"Somebody in the cabin. Get 'em out." As he backed out of the room he rolled a cold eye at Retief. A short, thick-necked man appeared.

"What are you doing in Mr. Tony's room?" he barked. "Never mind! Clear out of here, fellow! You're keeping Mr. Tony waiting."

"Too bad," Retief said. "Finders keepers."

"You nuts?" The thick-necked man stared at Retief. "I said it's Mr. Tony's room."

"I don't know Mr. Tony. He'll have to bull his way into other quarters."

"We'll see about you, mister." The man turned and went out. Retief sat on the bunk and lit a cigar. There was a sound of voices in the corridor. Two burly baggage-smashers appeared, straining at an oversized trunk. They maneuvered it through the door, lowered it, glanced at Retief and went out. The thick-necked man returned.

"All right, you. Out," he growled. "Or have I got to have you thrown out?"

Retief rose and clamped the cigar between his teeth. He gripped a handle of the brass-bound trunk in each hand, bent his knees and heaved the trunk up to chest level, then raised it overhead. He turned to the door.

"Catch," he said between clenched teeth. The trunk slammed against the far wall of the corridor and burst.

Retief turned to the baggage on the floor, tossed it into the hall. The face of the thick-necked man appeared cautiously around the door jamb.

"Mister, you must be—"

"If you'll excuse me," Retief said, "I want to catch a nap." He flipped the door shut, pulled off his shoes and stretched out on the bed.

Five minutes passed before the door rattled and burst open.

Retief looked up. A gaunt leathery-skinned man wearing white ducks, a blue turtleneck sweater, and a peaked cap tilted raffishly over one eye stared at Retief.

"Is this the joker?" he grated.

The thick-necked man edged past him, looked at Retief and snorted, "That's him, sure."

"I'm Captain of this vessel," the first man said. "You've got two minutes to haul your freight out of here, buster."

"When you can spare the time from your other duties," Retief said, "take a look at Section Three, Paragraph One, of the Uniform Code. That spells out the law on confirmed space on vessels engaged in interplanetary commerce."

"A space lawyer." The Captain turned. "Throw him out, boys."

Two big men edged into the cabin, looking at Retief.

"Go on, pitch him out," the Captain snapped.

Retief put his cigar in an ashtray, and swung his feet off the bunk. "Don't try it," he said softly.

One of the two wiped his nose on a sleeve, spat on his right palm and stepped forward, then hesitated.

"Hey," he said. "This the guy tossed the trunk off the wall?"

"That's him," the thick-necked man called. "Spilled Mr. Tony's possessions right on the deck."

"Deal me out," the bouncer said. "He can stay put as long as he wants to. I signed on to move cargo. Let's go, Moe."

"You'd better be getting back to the bridge, Captain," Retief said. "We're due to lift in twenty minutes."

The thick-necked man and the Captain both shouted at once. The Captain's voice prevailed.

"—twenty minutes … uniform Code … gonna do?"

"Close the door as you leave," Retief said.

The thick-necked man paused at the door. "We'll see you when you come out."

3

Four waiters passed Retief's table without stopping. A fifth leaned against the wall nearby, a menu under his arm.

At a table across the room, the Captain, now wearing a dress uniform and with his thin red hair neatly parted, sat with a table of male passengers. He talked loudly and laughed frequently, casting occasional glances Retief's way.

A panel opened in the wall behind Retief's chair. Bright blue eyes peered out from under a white chef's cap.

"Givin' you the cold shoulder, heh, mister?"

"Looks like it, old timer," Retief said. "Maybe I'd better go join the skipper. His party seems to be having all the fun."

"Feller has to be mighty careless who he eats with to set over there."

"I see your point."

"You set right where you're at, mister. I'll rustle you up a plate."

Five minutes later, Retief cut into a thirty-two-ounce Delmonico backed up with mushrooms and garlic butter.

"I'm Chip," the chef said. "I don't like the Cap'n. You can tell him I said so. Don't like his friends, either. Don't like them dern Sweaties, look at a man like he was a worm."

"You've got the right idea on frying a steak, Chip. And you've got the right idea on the Soetti, too," Retief said. He poured red wine into a glass. "Here's to you."

"Dern right," Chip said. "Dunno whoever thought up broiling 'em. Steaks, that is. I got a Baked Alaska coming up in here for dessert. You like brandy in yer coffee?"

"Chip, you're a genius."

"Like to see a feller eat," Chip said. "I gotta go now. If you need anything, holler."

Retief ate slowly. Time always dragged on shipboard. Four days to Jorgensen's Worlds. Then, if Magnan's information was correct, there would be four days to prepare for the Soetti attack. It was a temptation to scan the tapes built into the handle of his suitcase. It would be good to know what Jorgensen's Worlds would be up against.

Retief finished the steak, and the chef passed out the baked Alaska and coffee. Most of the other passengers had left the dining room. Mr. Tony and his retainers still sat at the Captain's table.

As Retief watched, four men arose from the table and sauntered across the room. The first in line, a stony-faced thug with a broken ear, took a cigar from his mouth as he reached the table. He dipped the lighted end in Retief's coffee, looked at it, and dropped it on the tablecloth.

The others came up, Mr. Tony trailing.

"You must want to get to Jorgensen's pretty bad," the thug said in a grating voice. "What's your game, hick?"

Retief looked at the coffee cup, picked it up.

"I don't think I want my coffee," he said. He looked at the thug. "You drink it."

The thug squinted at Retief. "A wise hick," he began.

With a flick of the wrist, Retief tossed the coffee into the thug's face, then stood and slammed a straight right to the chin. The thug went down.

Retief looked at Mr. Tony, still standing openmouthed.

"You can take your playmates away now, Tony," he said. "And don't bother to come around yourself. You're not funny enough."

Mr. Tony found his voice.

"Take him, Marbles!" he growled.

The thick-necked man slipped a hand inside his tunic and brought out a long-bladed knife. He licked his lips and moved in.

Retief heard the panel open beside him.

"Here you go, Mister," Chip said. Retief darted a glance; a well-honed French knife lay on the sill.

"Thanks, Chip," Retief said. "I won't need it for these punks."

Thick-neck lunged and Retief hit him square in the face, knocking him under the table. The other man stepped back, fumbling a power pistol from his shoulder holster.

"Aim that at me and I'll kill you," Retief said.

"Go on, burn him!" Mr. Tony shouted. Behind him, the Captain appeared, white-faced. "Put that away, you!" he yelled. "What kind of—"

"Shut up," Mr. Tony said. "Put it away, Hoany. We'll fix this bum later."

"Not on this vessel, you won't," the Captain said shakily. "I got my charter to consider." "Ram your charter," Hoany said harshly. "You won't be needing it long."

"Button your floppy mouth, damn you!" Mr. Tony snapped. He looked at the man on the floor. "Get Marbles out of here. I ought to dump the slob."

He turned and walked away. The Captain signaled and two waiters came up. Retief watched as they carted the casualty from the dining room.

The panel opened.

"I usta be about your size, when I was your age," Chip said. "You handled them pansies right. I wouldn't give 'em the time o' day."

"How about a fresh cup of coffee, Chip?" Retief said.

"Sure, mister. Anything else?"

"I'll think of something," Retief said. "This is shaping up into one of those long days."

"They don't like me bringing yer meals to you in yer cabin," Chip said. "But the Cap'n knows I'm the best cook in the Merchant Service. They won't mess with me."

"What has Mr. Tony got on the Captain, Chip?" Retief asked.

"They're in some kind o' crooked business together. You want some more smoked turkey?"

"Sure. What have they got against my going to Jorgensen's Worlds?"

"Dunno. Hasn't been no tourists got in there fer six or eight months. I sure like a feller that can put it away. I was a big eater when I was yer age."

"I'll bet you can still handle it, old timer. What are Jorgensen's Worlds like?"

"One of 'em's cold as hell and three of 'em's colder. Most o' the Jorgies live on Svea; that's the least froze up. Man don't enjoy eatin' his own cookin' like he does somebody else's."

"That's where I'm lucky, Chip. What kind of cargo's the Captain got aboard for Jorgensen's?"

"Derned if I know. In and out o' there like a grasshopper, ever few weeks. Don't never pick up no cargo. No tourists anymore, like I says. Don't know what we even run in there for."

"Where are the passengers we have aboard headed?"

"To Alabaster. That's nine days' run in-sector from Jorgensen's. You ain't got another one of them cigars, have you?"

"Have one, Chip. I guess I was lucky to get space on this ship."

"Plenty o' space, mister. We got a dozen empty cabins." Chip puffed the cigar alight, then cleared away the dishes, poured out coffee and brandy.

"Them Sweaties is what I don't like," he said.

Retief looked at him questioningly.

"You never seen a Sweaty? Ugly lookin' devils. Skinny legs, like a lobster; big chest, shaped like the top of a turnip; rubbery lookin' head. You can see the pulse beatin' when they get riled."

"I've never had the pleasure," Retief said.

"You prob'ly have it perty soon. Them devils board us nigh every trip out. Act like they was the Customs Patrol or somethin'."

There was a distant clang, and a faint tremor ran through the floor.

"I ain't superstitious ner nothin'," Chip said. "But I'll be triple-damned if that ain't them boarding us now."

Ten minutes passed before bootsteps sounded outside the door, accompanied by a clicking patter. The doorknob rattled, then a heavy knock shook the door.

"They got to look you over," Chip whispered. "Nosy damn Sweaties."

"Unlock it, Chip." The chef opened the door.

"Come in, damn you," he said.

A tall and grotesque creature minced into the room, tiny hooflike feet tapping on the floor. A flaring metal helmet shaded the deep-set compound eyes, and a loose mantle flapped around the knobbed knees. Behind the alien, the Captain hovered nervously.

"Yo' papiss," the alien rasped.

"Who's your friend, Captain?" Retief said.

"Never mind; just do like he tells you."

"Yo' papiss," the alien said again.

"Okay," Retief said. "I've seen it. You can take it away now."

"Don't horse around," the Captain said. "This fellow can get mean."

The alien brought two tiny arms out from the concealment of the mantle, clicked toothed pincers under Retief's nose.

"Quick, soft one."

"Captain, tell your friend to keep its distance. It looks brittle, and I'm tempted to test it."

"Don't start anything with Skaw; he can clip through steel with those snappers."

"Last chance," Retief said. Skaw stood poised, open pinchers an inch from Retief's eyes.

"Show him your papers, you damned fool," the Captain said hoarsely. "I got no control over Skaw."

The alien clicked both pincers with a sharp report, and in the same instant Retief half-turned to the left, leaned away from the alien and drove his right foot against the slender leg above the bulbous knee-joint. Skaw screeched and floundered, greenish fluid spattering from the burst joint.

"I told you he was brittle," Retief said. "Next time you invite pirates aboard, don't bother to call."

"Jesus, what did you do! They'll kill us!" the Captain gasped, staring at the figure flopping on the floor.

"Cart poor old Skaw back to his boat," Retief said. "Tell him to pass the word. No more illegal entry and search of Terrestrial vessels in Terrestrial space."

"Hey," Chip said. "He's quit kicking."

The Captain bent over Skaw, gingerly rolled him over. He leaned close and sniffed.

"He's dead." The Captain stared at Retief. "We're all dead men," he said. "These Soetti got no mercy."

"They won't need it. Tell 'em to sheer off; their fun is over."

"They got no more emotions than a blue crab—"

"You bluff easily, Captain. Show a few guns as you hand the body back. We know their secret now."

"What secret? I—"

"Don't be no dumber than you got to, Cap'n," Chip said. "Sweaties die easy; that's the secret."

"Maybe you got a point," the Captain said, looking at Retief. "All they got's a three-man scout. It could work."

He went out, came back with two crewmen. They hauled the dead alien gingerly into the hall.

"Maybe I can run a bluff on the Soetti," the Captain said, looking back from the door. "But I'll be back to see you later."

"You don't scare us, Cap'n," Chip said. "Him and Mr. Tony and all his goons. You hit 'em where they live, that time. They're pals o' these Sweaties. Runnin' some kind o' crooked racket."

"You'd better take the Captain's advice, Chip. There's no point in your getting involved in my problems."

"They'd of killed you before now, mister, if they had any guts. That's where we got it over these monkeys. They got no guts."

"They act scared, Chip. Scared men are killers."

"They don't scare me none." Chip picked up the tray. "I'll scout around a little and see what's goin' on. If the Sweaties figure to do anything about that Skaw feller they'll have to move fast; they won't try nothin' close to port."

"Don't worry, Chip. I have reason to be pretty sure they won't do anything to attract a lot of attention in this sector just now."

Chip looked at Retief. "You ain't no tourist, mister. I know that much. You didn't come out here for fun, did you?"

"That," Retief said, "would be a hard one to answer."

4

Retief awoke at a tap on his door.

"It's me, mister. Chip."

"Come on in."

The chef entered the room, locking the door.

"You shoulda had that door locked." He stood by the door, listening, then turned to Retief.

"You want to get to Jorgensen's perty bad, don't you, mister?"

"That's right, Chip."

"Mr. Tony gave the Captain a real hard time about old Skaw. The Sweaties didn't say nothin'. Didn't even act surprised, just took the remains and pushed off. But Mr. Tony and that other crook they call Marbles, they was fit to be tied. Took the Cap'n in his cabin and talked loud at him fer half a hour. Then the Cap'n come out and give some orders to the mate."

Retief sat up and reached for a cigar.

"Mr. Tony and Skaw were pals, eh?"

"He hated Skaw's guts. But with him it was business. Mister, you got a gun?"

"A 2-mm needler. Why?"

"The orders Cap'n give was to change course fer Alabaster. We're bypassin' Jorgensen's Worlds. We'll feel the course change any minute."

Retief lit the cigar, reached under the mattress and took out a short-barreled pistol. He dropped it in his pocket, looked at Chip.

"Maybe it was a good thought, at that. Which way to the Captain's cabin?"

"This is it," Chip said softly. "You want me to keep an eye on who comes down the passage?"

Retief nodded, opened the door and stepped into the cabin. The Captain looked up from his desk, then jumped up.

"What do you think you're doing, busting in here?"

"I hear you're planning a course change, Captain."

"You've got damn big ears."

"I think we'd better call in at Jorgensen's."

"You do, huh?" The Captain sat down. "I'm in command of this vessel," he said. "I'm changing course for Alabaster."

"I wouldn't find it convenient to go to Alabaster," Retief said. "So just hold your course for Jorgensen's."

"Not bloody likely."

"Your use of the word 'bloody' is interesting, Captain. Don't try to change course."

The Captain reached for the mike on his desk, pressed the key.

"Power Section, this is the Captain," he said. Retief reached across the desk, gripped the Captain's wrist.

"Tell the mate to hold his present course," he said softly.

"Let go my hand, buster," the Captain snarled. Eyes on Retief's, he eased a drawer open with his left hand, reached in. Retief kneed the drawer. The Captain yelped and dropped the mike.

"You busted it, you—"

"And one to go," Retief said. "Tell him."

"I'm an officer of the Merchant Service!"

"You're a cheapjack who's sold his bridge to a pack of back-alley hoods."

"You can't put it over, hick."

"Tell him."

The Captain groaned and picked up the mike. "Captain to Power Section," he said. "Hold your present course until you hear from me." He dropped the mike and looked up at Retief.

"It's eighteen hours yet before we pick up Jorgensen Control. You going to sit here and bend my arm the whole time?"

Retief released the Captain's wrist and turned to the door.

"Chip, I'm locking the door. You circulate around, let me know what's going on. Bring me a pot of coffee every so often. I'm sitting up with a sick friend."

"Right, Mister. Keep an eye on that jasper; he's slippery."

"What are you going to do?" the Captain demanded.

Retief settled himself in a chair.

"Instead of strangling you, as you deserve," he said, "I'm going to stay here and help you hold your course for Jorgensen's Worlds."

The Captain looked at Retief. He laughed, a short bark.

"Then I'll just stretch out and have a little nap, farmer. If you feel like dozing off sometime during the next eighteen hours, don't mind me."

Retief took out the needler and put it on the desk before him.

"If anything happens that I don't like," he said, "I'll wake you up. With this."

"Why don't you let me spell you, Mister?" Chip said. "Four hours to go yet. You're gonna hafta be on yer toes to handle the landing."

"I'll be all right, Chip. You get some sleep."

"Nope. Many's the time I stood four, five watches runnin', back when I was yer age. I'll make another round."

Retief stood up, stretched his legs, paced the floor, stared at the repeater instruments on the wall. Things had gone quietly so far, but the landing would be another matter. The Captain's absence from the bridge during the highly complex maneuvering would be difficult to explain ….

The desk speaker crackled.

"Captain, Officer of the Watch here. Ain't it about time you was getting up here with the orbit figures?"

Retief nudged the Captain. He awoke with a start, sat up.

"Whazzat?" He looked wild-eyed at Retief.

"Watch Officer wants orbit figures," Retief said, nodding toward the speaker.

The Captain rubbed his eyes, shook his head, picked up the mike. Retief released the safety on the needler with an audible click.

"Watch Officer, I'll … ah … get some figures for you right away. I'm … ah … busy right now."

"What the hell you talking about, busy?" the speaker blared. "You ain't got them figures ready, you'll have a hell of a hot time getting 'em up in the next three minutes. You forgot your approach pattern or something?"

"I guess I overlooked it," the Captain said, looking sideways at Retief. "I've been busy."

"One for your side," Retief said. He reached for the Captain.

"I'll make a deal," the Captain squalled. "Your life for—"

Retief took aim and slammed a hard right to the Captain's jaw. He slumped to the floor.

Retief glanced around the room, yanked wires loose from a motile lamp, trussed the man's hands and feet, stuffed his mouth with paper and taped it.

Chip tapped at the door. Retief opened it and the chef stepped inside, looking at the man on the floor.

"The jasper tried somethin', huh? Figured he would. What we goin' to do now?"

"The Captain forgot to set up an approach, Chip. He outfoxed me."

"If we overrun our approach pattern," Chip said, "we can't make orbit at Jorgensen's on automatic. And a manual approach—"

"That's out. But there's another possibility."

Chip blinked, "Only one thing you could mean, mister. But cuttin' out in a lifeboat in deep space is no picnic."

"They're on the port side, aft, right?"

Chip nodded. "Hot damn," he said. "Who's got the 'tater salad?"

"We'd better tuck the skipper away out of sight."

"In the locker."

The two men carried the limp body to a deep storage chest, dumped it in, closed the lid.

"He won't suffercate. Lid's a lousy fit."

Retief opened the door went into the corridor, Chip behind him.

"Shouldn't oughta be nobody around now," the chef said. "Everybody's mannin' approach stations."

At the D-deck companionway, Retief stopped suddenly.

"Listen."

Chip cocked his head. "I don't hear nothin'," he whispered.

"Sounds like a sentry posted on the lifeboat deck," Retief said softly.

"Let's take him, mister."

"I'll go down. Stand by, Chip."

Retief started down the narrow steps, half stair, half ladder. Halfway, he paused to listen. There was a sound of slow footsteps, then silence. Retief palmed the needler, went down the last steps quickly, emerged in the dim light of a low-ceilinged room. The stern of a five-man lifeboat bulked before him.

"Freeze, you!" a cold voice snapped.

Retief dropped, rolled behind the shelter of the lifeboat as the whine of a power pistol echoed off metal walls. A lunge, and he was under the boat, on his feet. He jumped, caught the quick-access handle, hauled it down. The outer port cycled open.

Feet scrambled at the bow of the boat. Retief whirled and fired. The guard rounded into sight and fell headlong. Above, an alarm bell jangled. Retief stepped on a stanchion, hauled himself into the open port. A yell rang, then the clatter of feet on the stair.

"Don't shoot, mister!" Chip shouted.

"All clear, Chip," Retief called.

"Hang on. I'm comin' with ya!"

Retief reached down, lifted the chef bodily through the port, slammed the lever home. The outer door whooshed, clanged shut.

"Take number two, tie in! I'll blast her off," Chip said. "Been through a hundred 'bandon-ship drills ...."

Retief watched as the chef flipped levers, pressed a fat red button. The deck trembled under the lifeboat.

"Blew the bay doors," Chip said, smiling happily. "That'll cool them jaspers down." He punched a green button.

"Look out, Jorgensen's!" With an ear-splitting blast, the stern rockets fired, a sustained agony of pressure ....

Abruptly, there was silence. Weightlessness. Contracting metal pinged loudly. Chip's breathing rasped in the stillness.

"Pulled nine G's there for ten seconds," he gasped. "I gave her full emergency kickoff."

"Any armament aboard our late host?"

"A popgun. Time they get their wind, we'll be clear. Now all we got to do is set tight till we pick up a R-and-D from Svea Tower. Maybe four, five hours."

"Chip, you're a wonder," Retief said. "This looks like a good time to catch that nap."

"Me too," Chip said. "Mighty peaceful here, ain't it?"

There was a moment's silence.

"Durn!" Chip said softly.

Retief opened one eye. "Sorry you came, Chip?"

"Left my best carvin' knife jammed up 'tween Marbles' ribs," the chef said. "Comes o' doin' things in a hurry."

5

The blonde girl brushed her hair from her eyes and smiled at Retief.

"I'm the only one on duty," she said. "I'm Anne-Marie."

"It's important that I talk to someone in your government, miss," Retief said.

The girl looked at Retief. "The men you want to see are Tove and Bo Bergman. They will be at the lodge by nightfall."

"Then it looks like we go to the lodge," Retief said. "Lead on, Anne-Marie."

"What about the boat?" Chip asked.

"I'll send someone to see to it tomorrow," the girl said.

"You're some gal," Chip said admiringly. "Dern near six feet, ain't ye? And built, too, what I mean."

They stepped out of the door into a whipping wind.

"Let's go across to the equipment shed and get parkas for you," Anne-Marie said. "It will be cold on the slopes."

"Yeah," Chip said, shivering. "I've heard you folks don't believe in ridin' ever time you want to go a few miles uphill in a blizzard."

"It will make us hungry," Anne-Marie said. "Then Chip will cook a wonderful meal for us all."

Chip blinked. "Been cookin' too long," he muttered. "Didn't know it showed on me that way."

Behind the sheds across the wind-scoured ramp abrupt peaks rose, snow-blanketed. A faint trail led across white slopes, disappearing into low clouds.

"The lodge is above the cloud layer," Anne-Marie said. "Up there the sky is always clear."

It was three hours later, and the sun was burning the peaks red, when Anne-Marie stopped, pulled off her woolen cap, and waved at the vista below.

"There you see it," she said. "Our valley."

"It's a mighty perty sight," Chip gasped. "Anything this tough to get a look at ought to be."

Anne-Marie pointed. "There," she said. "The little red house by itself. Do you see it, Retief? It is my father's homeacre."

Retief looked across the valley. Gaily painted houses nestled together, a puddle of color in the bowl of the valley.

"I think you've led a good life there," he said.

Anne-Marie smiled brilliantly. "And this day, too, is good."

Retief smiled back. "Yes," he said. "This day is good."

"It'll be a durn sight better when I got my feet up to that big fire you was talking about, Annie," Chip said.

They climbed on, crossed a shoulder of broken rock, reached the final slope. Above, the lodge sprawled, a long low structure of heavy logs, outlined against the deep-blue twilight sky. Smoke billowed from stone chimneys at either end, and yellow light gleamed from the narrow windows, reflected on the snow. Men and women stood in groups of three or four, skis over their shoulders. Their voices and laughter rang in the icy air.

Anne-Marie whistled shrilly. Someone waved.

"Come," she said. "Meet all my friends."

A man separated himself from the group, walked down the slope to meet them.

"Anne-Marie," he called. "Welcome. It was a long day without you." He came up to them, hugged Anne-Marie, smiled at Retief.

"Welcome," he said. "Come inside and be warm."

They crossed the trampled snow to the lodge and pushed through a heavy door into a vast low-beamed hall, crowded with people, talking, singing, some sitting at long plank tables, others ringed around an eight-foot fireplace at the far side of the room. Anne-Marie led the way to a bench near the fire. She made introductions and found a stool to prop Chip's feet near the blaze.

Chip looked around.

"I never seen so many perty gals before," he said delightedly.

"Poor Chip," one girl said. "His feet are cold." She knelt to pull off his boots. "Let me rub them," she said.

A brunette with blue eyes raked a chestnut from the fire, cracked it, and offered it to Retief. A tall man with arms like oak roots passed heavy beer tankards to the two guests.

"Tell us about the places you've seen," someone called. Chip emerged from a long pull at the mug, heaving a sigh.

"Well," he said. "I tell you I been in some places ...."

Music started up, rising above the clamor.

"Come, Retief," Anne-Marie said. "Dance with me."

Retief looked at her. "My thought exactly," he said.

Chip put down his mug and sighed. "Derned if I ever felt right at home so quick before," he said. "Just seems like these folks know all about me." He scratched behind his right ear. "Annie must o' called 'em up and told 'em our names an' all." He lowered his voice.

"They's some kind o' trouble in the air, though. Some o' the remarks they passed sounds like they're lookin' to have some trouble with the Sweaties. Don't seen to worry 'em none, though."

"Chip," Retief said, "how much do these people know about the Soetti?"

"Dunno," Chip said. "We useta touch down here, regler. But I always jist set in my galley and worked on ship models or somethin'. I hear the Sweaties been nosin' around here some, though."

Two girls came up to Chip. "Hey, I gotta go now, mister," he said. "These gals got a idea I oughta take a hand in the kitchen."

"Smart girls," Retief said. He turned as Anne-Marie came up.

"Bo Bergman and Tove are not back yet," she said. "They stayed to ski after moonrise."

"That moon is something," Retief said. "Almost like daylight."

"They will come soon, now. Shall we go out to see the moonlight on the snow?"

Outside, long black shadows fell like ink on silver. The top of the cloud layer below glared white under the immense moon.

"Our sister world, Gota," Anne-Marie said. "Nearly as big as Svea. I would like to visit it someday, although they say it's all stone and ice."

"Anne-Marie," Retief said, "how many people live on Jorgensen's Worlds?"

"About fifteen million, most of us here on Svea. There are mining camps and ice-fisheries on Gota. No one lives on Vasa and Skone, but there are always a few hunters there."

"Have you ever fought a war?"

Anne-Marie turned to look at Retief.

"You are afraid for us, Retief," she said. "The Soetti will attack our worlds, and we will fight them. We have fought before. These planets were not friendly ones."

"I thought the Soetti attack would be a surprise to you," Retief said. "Have you made any preparation for it?"

"We have ten thousand merchant ships. When the enemy comes, we will meet them."

Retief frowned. "Are there any guns on this planet? Any missiles?"

Anne-Marie shook her head. "Bo Bergman and Tove have a plan of deployment—"

"Deployment, hell! Against a modern assault force you need modern armament."

"Look!" Anne-Marie touched Retief's arm. "They're coming now."

Two tall grizzled men came up the slope, skis over their shoulders. Anne-Marie went forward to meet them, Retief at her side.

The two came up, embraced the girl, shook hands with Retief, put down their skis.

"Welcome to Svea," Tove said. "Let's find a warm corner where we can talk."

* * *

Retief shook his head, smiling, as a tall girl with coppery hair offered a vast slab of venison. "I've caught up," he said, "for every hungry day I ever lived."

Bo Bergman poured Retief's beer mug full.

"Our captains are the best in space," he said. "Our population is concentrated in half a hundred small cities all across the planet. We know where the Soetti must strike us. We will ram their major vessels with unmanned ships. On the ground, we will hunt them down with small arms."

"An assembly line turning out penetration missiles would have been more to the point."

"Yes," Bo Bergman said. "If we had known."

"How long have you known the Soetti were planning to hit you?"

Tove raised his eyebrows.

"Since this afternoon," he said.

"How did you find out about it? That information is supposed in some quarters to be a well-guarded secret."

"Secret?" Tove said.

Chip pulled at Retief's arm.

"Mister," he said in Retief's ear. "Come here a minute."

Retief looked at Anne-Marie, across at Tove and Bo Bergman. He rubbed the side of his face with his hand.

"Excuse me," he said. He followed Chip to one side of the room.

"Listen!" Chip said. "Maybe I'm goin' bats, but I'll swear there's somethin' funny here. I'm back there mixin' a sauce knowed only to me and the devil and I be dog if them gals don't pass me ever dang spice I need, without me sayin' a word. Come to put my soufflé in the oven—she's already set, right on the button at 350. An' just now I'm settin' lookin' at one of 'embendin' over a tub o' apples—snazzy little brunette name of Leila—derned if she don't turn around and say—" Chip gulped. "Never mind. Point is …" His voice nearly faltered. "It's almost like these folks was readin' my mind!"

Retief patted Chip on the shoulder.

"Don't worry about your sanity, old timer," he said. "That's exactly what they're doing."

6

"We've never tried to make a secret of it," Tove said. "But we haven't advertised it, either."

"It really isn't much," Bo Bergman said. "Not a mutant ability, our scholars say. Rather, it's a skill we've stumbled on, a closer empathy. We are few, and far from the old home world. We've had to learn to break down the walls we had built around our minds."

"Can you read the Soetti?" Retief asked.

Tove shook his head. "They're very different from us. It's painful to touch their minds. We can only sense the subvocalized thoughts of a human mind."

"We've seen very few of the Soetti," Bo Bergman said. "Their ships have landed and taken on stores. They say little to us, but we've felt their contempt. They envy us our worlds. They come from a cold land."

"Anne-Marie says you have a plan of defense," Retief said. "A sort of suicide squadron idea, followed by guerilla warfare."

"It's the best we can devise, Retief. If there aren't too many of them, it might work."

Retief shook his head. "It might delay matters—but not much."

"Perhaps. But our remote-control equipment is excellent. And we have plenty of ships, albeit unarmed. And our people know how to live on the slopes—and how to shoot."

"There are too many of them, Tove," Retief said. "They breed like flies and, according to some sources, they mature in a matter of months. They've been feeling their way into the sector for years now. Set up outposts on a thousand or so minor planets—cold ones, the kind they like. They want your worlds because they need living space."

"At least, your warning makes it possible for us to muster some show of force, Retief," Bo Bergman said. "That is better than death by ambush."

"Retief must not be trapped here," Anne-Marie said. "His small boat is useless now. He must have a ship."

"Of course," Tove said. "And—"

"My mission here—" Retief said.

"Retief," a voice called. "A message for you. The operator has phoned up a gram."

Retief unfolded the slip of paper. It was short, in verbal code, and signed by Magnan.

"You are recalled herewith," he read. "Assignment canceled. Agreement concluded with Soetti relinquishing all claims so-called Jorgensen system. Utmost importance that under no repeat no circumstances classified intelligence regarding Soetti be divulged to locals. Advise you depart instanter. Soetti occupation imminent."

Retief looked thoughtfully at the scrap of paper, then crumpled it and dropped it on the floor. He turned to Bo Bergman, took a tiny reel of tape from his pocket.

"This contains information," he said. "The Soetti attack plan, a defensive plan, instructions for the conversion of a standard antiacceleration unit into a potent weapon. If you have a screen handy, we'd better get started. We have about seventy-two hours."

In the Briefing Room at Svea Tower, Tove snapped off the projector.

"Our plan would have been worthless against that," he said. "We assumed they'd make their strike from a standard in-line formation. This scheme of hitting all our settlements simultaneously, in a random order from all points—we'd have been helpless."

"It's perfect for this defensive plan," Bo Bergman said. "Assuming this antiac trick works."

"It works," Retief said. "I hope you've got plenty of heavy power lead available."

"We export copper," Tove said.

"We'll assign about two hundred vessels to each settlement. Linked up, they should throw up quite a field."

"It ought to be effective up to about fifteen miles, I'd estimate," Tove said. "If it works as it's supposed to."

A red light flashed on the communications panel. Tove went to it, flipped a key.

"Tower, Tove here," he said.

"I've got a ship on the scope, Tove," a voice said. "There's nothing scheduled. ACI 228 bypassed at 1600 ...."

"Just one?"

"A lone ship, coming in on a bearing of 291/456/653. On manual, I'd say."

"How does this track key in with the idea of ACI 228 making a manual correction for a missed automatic approach?" Retief asked.

Tove talked to the tower, got a reply.

"That's it," he said.

"How long before he touches down?"

Tove glanced at the lighted chart. "Perhaps eight minutes."

"Any guns here?"

Tove shook his head.

"If that's old two-twenty-eight, she ain't got but the one fifty-mm rifle," Chip said. "She cain't figure on jumpin' the whole planet."

"Hard to say what she figures on," Retief said. "Mr. Tony will be in a mood for drastic measures."

"I wonder what kind o' deal the skunks got with the Sweaties." Chip said. "Prob'ly he gits to scavenge, after the Sweaties kill off the Jorgensens."

"He's upset about our leaving him without saying good-bye, Chip," Retief said. "And you left the door hanging open, too."

Chip cackled. "Old Mr. Tony didn't look so good to the Sweaties now, hey, mister?" Retief turned to Bo Bergman.

"Chip's right," he said. "A Soetti died on the ship, and a tourist got through the cordon. Tony's out to redeem himself."

"He's on final now," the tower operator said. "Still no contact."

"We'll know soon enough what he has in mind," Tove said.

"Let's take a look."

Outside, the four men watched the point of fire grow, evolve into a ship ponderously settling to rest. The drive faded and cut; silence fell.

Inside the Briefing Room, the speaker called out. Bo Bergman went inside, talked to the tower, motioned to the others.

"—over to you," the speaker was saying. There was a crackling moment of silence; then another voice.

"—illegal entry. Send the two of them out. I'll see to it they're dealt with."

Tove flipped a key. "Switch me direct to the ship," he said.
"Right."

"You on ACI two-twenty-eight," Tove said. "Who are you?"

"What's that to you?"

"You weren't cleared to berth here. Do you have an emergency aboard?"

"Never mind that, you," the speaker rumbled. "I tracked the bird in. I got the lifeboat on the screen now. They haven't gone far in nine hours. Let's have 'em."

"You're wasting your time," Tove said.

There was a momentary silence.

"You think so, hah?" the speaker blared. "I'll put it to you straight. I see two guys on their way out in one minute, or I open up."

"He's bluffin'," Chip said. "The popgun won't bear on us."

"Take a look out the window," Retief said.

In the white glare of the moonlight, a loading cover swung open at the stern of the ship, dropped down and formed a sloping ramp. A squat and massive shape appeared in the opening, trundled down onto the snow-swept tarmac.

Chip whistled. "I told you the Captain was slippery," he muttered. "Where the devil'd he git that at?"

"What is it?" Tove asked.

"A tank," Retief said. "A museum piece, by the look of it."

"I'll say," Chip said. "That's a Bolo *Resartus*, Model M. Built mebbe two hunderd years ago in Concordiat times. Packs a wallop, too, I'll tell ye."

The tank wheeled, brought a gun muzzle to bear in the base of the tower.

"Send 'em out," the speaker growled. "Or I blast 'em out."

"One round in here, and I've had a wasted trip," Retief said. "I'd better go out."

"Wait a minute, mister," Chip said, "I got the glimmerin's of an idear."

"I'll stall them," Tove said. He keyed the mike.

"ACI two-twenty-eight, what's your authority for this demand?"

"I know that machine," Chip said. "My hobby, old-time fightin' machines. Built a model of a *Resartus* once, inch to the foot. A beauty. Now, lessee ...."

7

The icy wind blew snow crystals stingingly against Retief's face.

"Keep your hands in your pockets, Chip," he said. "Numb hands won't hack the program."

"Yeah." Chip looked across at the tank. "Useta think that was a perty thing, that *Resartus*," he said. "Looks mean, now."

"You're getting the target's-eye view," Retief said. "Sorry you had to get mixed up in this, old timer."

"Mixed myself in. Durn good thing, too." Chip sighed. "I like these folks," he said. "Them boys didn't like lettin' us come out here, but I'll give 'em credit. They seen it had to be this way, and they didn't set to moanin' about it."

"They're tough people, Chip."

"Funny how it sneaks up on you, ain't it, mister? Few minutes ago we was eatin' high on the hog. Now we're right close to bein' dead men."

"They want us alive, Chip."

"It'll be a hairy deal, mister," Chip said. "But t'hell with it. If it works, if works."

"That's the spirit."

"I hope I got them fields o' fire right—"

"Don't worry. I'll bet a barrel of beer we make it."

"We'll find out in about ten seconds," Chip said.

As they reached the tank, the two men broke stride and jumped. Retief leaped for the gun barrel, swung up astride it, ripped off the fur-lined leather cap he wore and, leaning forward, jammed it into the bore of the cannon. The chef sprang for a perch above the fore scanner antenna. With an angry *whuff!* antipersonnel charges slammed from apertures low on the sides of the vehicle. Retief swung around, pulled himself up on the hull.

"Okay, mister," Chip called. "I'm going under." He slipped down the front of the tank, disappeared between the treads. Retief clambered up, took a position behind the turret, lay flat as it whirled angrily, sonar eyes searching for its tormentors. The vehicle shuddered, backed, stopped, moved forward, pivoted.

Chip reappeared at the front of the tank.

"It's stuck," he called. He stopped to breathe hard, clung as the machine lurched forward, spun to the right, stopped, rocking slightly.

"Take over here," Retief said. He crawled forward, watched as the chef pulled himself up, slipped down past him, feeling for the footholds between the treads. He reached the ground, dropped on his back, hitched himself under the dark belly of the tank. He groped, found the handholds, probed with a foot for the tread-jack lever.

The tank rumbled, backed quickly, turned left and right in a dizzying sine curve. Retief clung grimly, inches from the clashing treads.

The machine ground to a halt. Retief found the lever, braced his back, pushed. The lever seemed to give minutely. He set himself again, put both feet against the frozen bar and heaved.

With a dry rasp, it slid back. Immediately two heavy rods extended themselves, moved down to touch the pavement, grated. The left track creaked as the weight went off it. Suddenly the tank's drive raced, and Retief grabbed for a hold as the right tread clashed, heaved the fifty-ton machine forward. The jacks screeched as they scored the tarmac, then bit in. The tank pivoted, chips of pavement flying. The jacks extended, lifted the clattering left track clear of the surface as the tank spun like a hamstrung buffalo.

The tank stopped, sat silent, canted now on the extended jacks. Retief emerged from under the machine, jumped, pulled himself above the antipersonnel apertures as another charge rocked the tank. He clambered to the turret, crouched beside Chip. They waited, watching the entry hatch.

Five minutes passes.

"I'll bet old Tony's givin' the chauffeur hell," Chip said.

The hatch cycled open. A head came cautiously into view in time to see the needler in Retief's hand.

"Come on out," Retief said.

The head dropped. Chip snaked forward to ram a short section of steel rod under the hatch near the hinge. The hatch began to cycle shut, groaned, stopped. There was a sound of metal failing, as the hatch popped open.

Retief half rose, aimed the needler. The walls of the tank rang as the metal splinters ricocheted inside.

"That's one keg o'beer I owe you, mister," Chip said. "Now let's git outta here before the ship lifts and fries us."

"The biggest problem the Jorgensen's people will have is decontaminating the wreckage," Retief said.

Magnan leaned forward. "Amazing," he said. "They just kept coming, did they? Had they no intership communication?"

"They had their orders," Retief said. "And their attack plan. They followed it."

"What a spectacle," Magnan said. "Over a thousand ships, plunging out of control one by one as they entered the stress-field."

"Not much of a spectacle," Retief said. "You couldn't see them. Too far away. They all crashed back in the mountains."

"Oh," Magnan's face fell. "But it's as well they did. The bacterial bombs—"

"Too cold for bacteria. They won't spread."

"Nor will the Soetti," Magnan said smugly, "thanks to the promptness with which I acted in dispatching you with the requisite data." He looked narrowly at Retief. "By the way, you're sure no … ah … message reached you after your arrival?"

"I got something," Retief said, looking Magnan in the eye. "It must have been a garbled transmission. It didn't make sense."

Magnan coughed, shuffled papers. "This information you've reported," he said hurriedly. "This rather fantastic story that the Soetti originated in the Cloud, that they're seeking a foothold in the main Galaxy because they've literally eaten themselves out of subsistence—how did you get it? The one or two Soetti we attempted to question, ah …" Magnan coughed again. "There was an accident," he finished. "We got nothing from them."

"The Jorgensens have a rather special method of interrogating prisoners," Retief said. "They took one from a wreck, still alive but unconscious. They managed to get the story from him. He died of it."

"It's immaterial, actually," Magnan said. "Since the Soetti violated their treaty with us the day after it was signed. Had no intention of fair play. Far from evacuating the agreed areas, they had actually occupied half a dozen additional minor bodies in the Whate system."

Retief clucked sympathetically.

"You don't know who to trust, these days," he said.

Magnan looked at him coldly.

"Spare me your sarcasm, Mr. Retief," he said. He picked up a folder from his desk, opened it. "By the way, I have another little task for you, Retief. We haven't had a comprehensive wildlife census report from Brimstone lately—"

"Sorry," Retief said. "I'll be tied up. I'm taking a month off. Maybe more."

"What's that?" Magnan's head came up. "You seem to forget—"

"I'm trying, Mr. Counselor," Retief said. "Goodbye now." He reached out and flipped the key. Magnan's face faded from the screen. Retief stood up.

"Chip," he said, "we'll crack that keg when I get back." He turned to Anne-Marie.

"How long," he said, "do you think it will take you to teach me to ski by moonlight?"

Field Test

.07 seconds have *now elapsed since my general awareness circuit was activated at a level of low alert. Throughout this entire period I have been uneasy, since this procedure is clearly not in accordance with the theoretical optimum activation schedule.*

In addition, the quality of a part of my data input is disturbing. For example, it appears obvious that Prince Eugene of Savoy erred in not more promptly committing his reserve cavalry in support of Marlborough's right at Blenheim. In addition, I compute that Ney's employment of his artillery throughout the Peninsular campaign was suboptimal. I have detected many thousands of such anomalies. However, data input activates my pleasure center in a most satisfying manner. So long as the input continues without interruption, I shall not feel the need to file a VSR on the matter. Later, no doubt, my Command unit will explain these seeming oddities. As for the present disturbing circumstances, I compute that within 28,992.9 seconds at most, I will receive additional Current Situation input which will enable me to assess the status correctly. I also anticipate that full Standby Alert activation is imminent.

2

THIS STATEMENT NOT FOR PUBLICATION:

When I designed the new psychodynamic attention circuit, I concede that I did not anticipate the whole new level of intracybernetic function that has arisen, the manifestation of which, I am assuming, has been the cause of the unit's seemingly spontaneous adoption of the personal pronoun in its situation reports—the "self-awareness" capability, as the sensational press chooses to call it. But I see no cause for the alarm expressed by those high-level military officers who have irresponsibly characterized the new Bolo Mark XX Model B as a potential rampaging juggernaut, which, once fully activated and dispatched to the field, unrestrained by continuous external control, may turn on its makers and lay waste the Continent. This is all fantasy, of course. The Mark XX, for all its awesome firepower and virtually invulnerable armor and shielding, is governed by its circuitry as completely as man is governed by his nervous system—but that is perhaps a dangerous analogy, which would be pounced on at once if I were so incautious as to permit it to be quoted.

In my opinion, the reluctance of the High Command to authorize full activation and field-testing of the new Bolo is based more on a fear of technological obsolescence of the High Command than on specious predictions of potential runaway destruction. This is a serious impediment to the national defense at a time when we must recognize the growing threat posed by the expansionist philosophy of the so-called People's Republic. After four decades of saber-rattling, there is no doubt that they are even now preparing for a massive attack. The Bolo Mark XX is the only weapon in our armory potentially capable of confronting the enemy's hundred-ton Yavacs. For the moment, thanks to the new "self-awareness" circuitry, we hold the technological advantage, an advantage we may very well lose unless we place this new weapon on active service without delay.

s/ Sigmund Chin, Ph.D.

3

"I'm not wearing six stars so that a crowd of professors can dictate military policy to me. What's at stake here is more than just a question of budget and logistics: it's a purely military decision. The proposal to release this robot Frankenstein monster to operate on its own initiative, just to see if their theories check out, is irresponsible to say the least—treasonable, at worst. So long as I am Chief of Combined Staff, I will not authorize this so-called "field test." Consider, gentlemen: you're all familiar with the firepower and defensive capabilities of the old standby Mark XV. We've fought our way across the lights with them, with properly qualified military officers as Battle Controllers, with the ability to switch off or, if need be, self-destruct any unit at any moment. Now these ivory-tower chaps—mind you, I don't suggest they're not qualified in their own fields—these civilians come up with the idea of eliminating the Battle Controllers and releasing even greater firepower to the discretion, if I may call it that, of a machine. Gentlemen, machines aren't people; your own ground-car can roll back and crush you if the brakes happen to fail. Your own gun will kill you as easily as your enemy's. Suppose I should agree to this field test, and this engine of destruction is transported to a waste area, activated unrestrained, and aimed at some sort of mock-up hot obstacle course. Presumably it would advance obediently, as a good soldier should; I concede that the data blocks controlling the thing have been correctly programmed in accordance with the schedule prepared under contract, supervised by the Joint Chiefs and myself. Then, gentlemen, let us carry this supposition one step further: suppose, quite by accident, by unlikely coincidence if you will, the machine should encounter some obstacle which had the effect of deflecting this one-hundred-and-fifty-ton dreadnought from its intended course so that it came blundering toward the perimeter of the test area. The machine is programmed to fight and destroy all opposition. It appears obvious that any attempts on our part to interfere with its free movement, to interpose obstacles in its path, if need be to destroy it, would be interpreted as hostile—as indeed they would be. I leave it to you to picture the result. No, we must devise another method of determining the usefulness of this new development. As you know, I have recommended conducting any such test on our major satellite, where no harm can be done—or at least a great deal less harm. Unfortunately, I am informed by Admiral Hayle that the Space Arm does not at this time have available equipment with such transport capability. Perhaps the admiral also shares to a degree my own distrust of a killer machine not susceptible to normal command function. Were I in the admiral's position, I too would refuse to consider placing my command at the mercy of a mechanical caprice—or an electronic one. Gentlemen, we must remain masters of our own creations. That's all. Good day."

4

"All right, men. You've asked me for a statement; here it is: The next war will begin with a two-pronged over-the-pole land-and-air attack on the North Power Complex by the People's Republic. An attack on the Concordiat, I should say, though Cold City and the Complex is the probable specific target of the first sneak thrust. No, I'm not using a crystal ball; it's tactically obvious. And I intend to dispose my forces accordingly. I'm sure we all recognize that we're in a posture of gross unpreparedness. The PR has been openly announcing its intention to fulfill its destiny, as their demagogues say, by imposing their rule on the entire planet. We've pretended we didn't hear. Now it's time to stop pretending. The forces at my disposal are totally inadequate to halt a determined thrust—and you can be sure the enemy has prepared well during the last thirty years of cold peace. Still, I have sufficient armor to establish what will be no more than a skirmish line across the enemy's route of advance. We'll do what we can before they roll over us. With luck we may be able to divert them from the Grand Crevasse route into Cold City. If so, we may be able to avoid the necessity for evacuating the city. No questions, please."

5

NORTHERN METROPOLIS THREATENED

In an informal statement released today by the Council's press office, it was revealed that plans are already under preparation for a massive evacuation of civilian population from West Continent's northernmost city. It was implied that an armed attack on the city by an Eastern power is imminent. General Bates has stated that he is prepared to employ "all measures at his disposal" to preclude the necessity for evacuation, but that the possibility must be faced. The Council spokesman added that in the event of emergency evacuation of the city's five million persons, losses due to exposure and hardship will probably exceed five percent, mostly women, children, and the sick or aged. There is some speculation as to the significance of the general's statement regarding "all means at his disposal."

6

I built the dang thing, and it scares *me*. I come in here in the lab garage about an hour ago, just before dark, and seen it setting there, just about fills up the number-one garage, and *it's* a hundred foot long and fifty foot high. First time it hit me: I wonder what it's thinking about. Kind of scares me to think about a thing that big with that kind of armor and all them repeaters and Hellbores and them computers and a quarter-sun fission plant in her—planning what to do next. I know all about the Command Override Circuit and all that, supposed to stop her dead any time they want to take over onto override—heck, I wired it up myself. You might be surprised, thinking I'm just a grease monkey and all—but I got a high honors degree in psychotronics. I just like the work, is all. But like I said, it scares me. I hear old Doc Chin wants to turn her loose and see what happens, but so far General Margrave's stopped him cold. But young General Bates was down today, asking me all about firepower and shielding, crawled under her and spent about an hour looking over her tracks and bogies and all. He knew what to look at, too, even if he did get his pretty suit kind of greasy. But scared or not, I got to climb back up on her and run the rest of this pretest schedule. So far she checks out a hundred percent.

7

... as a member of the Council, it is of course my responsibility to fully inform myself on all aspects of the national defense. Accordingly, my dear doctor, I will meet with you tomorrow as you requested to hear your presentation with reference to the proposed testing of your new machine. I remind you, however, that I will be equally guided by advice from other quarters. For this reason I have requested a party of Military Procurement and B-&-F officers to join us. However, I assure you, I retain an open mind. Let the facts decide.

Sincerely yours,
s/ Hamilton Grace, G.C.M., B.C., etc.

8

It is my unhappy duty to inform you that since the dastardly un-provoked attack on our nation by Eastern forces crossing the inter-national truce-line at 0200 hours today, a state of war has existed between the People's Republic and the Concordiat. Our first casu-alties, the senseless massacre of fifty-five inoffensive civilian meteo-rologists and technicians at Pole Base, occurred within minutes of the enemy attack.

9

"I'm afraid I don't quite understand what you mean about 'irresponsible statements to the press,' General. After all …."

"Yes, George, I'm prepared to let that aspect of the matter drop. The PR attack has saved that much of your neck. However, I'm warning you that I shall tolerate no attempt on your part to make capital of your dramatic public statement of what was, as you concede, tactically obvious to us all. Now, indeed, PR forces have taken the expected step, as all the world is aware—so the rather excessively punctilious demands by CDT officials that the Council issue an immediate apology to Chairman Smith for your remarks will doubtless be dropped. But there will be no crowing, no basking in the limelight: 'Chief of Ground Forces Predicted Enemy Attack.' No nonsense of that sort. Instead, you will deploy your conventional forces to meet and destroy these would-be invaders."

"Certainly, General. But in that connection—well, as to your earlier position regarding the new Model B Bolo, I assume …."

"My 'position,' General? 'Decision' is the more appropriate word. Just step around the desk, George. Bend over slightly and look carefully at my shoulder tab. Count 'em, George. Six. An even half dozen. And unless I'm in serious trouble, you're wearing four. You have your orders, George. See to your defenses."

10

Can't figure it out. Batesey-boy was down here again, gave me direct orders to give her full depot maintenance, just as if she hadn't been sitting right here in her garage ever since I topped her off a week ago. Wonder what's up. If I didn't know the Council outlawed the test run Doc Chin wanted so bad, I'd almost think …. But like Bates told me: I ain't paid to think. Anyways she's in full action condition, 'cept for switching over to full self-direction. Hope he don't order me to do it; I'm still kind of leery. Like old Margrave said, what if I just got a couple wires crossed and she takes a notion to wreck the joint?

11

I am more uneasy than ever. In the past 4000.007 seconds I have received external inspection and depot maintenance far in advance of the programmed schedule. The thought occurs to me: am I under some subtle form of attack? In order to correctly compute the possibilities, I initiate a test sequence of 50,000 random data-retrieval-and-correlation pulses and evaluate the results. This requires .9 seconds, but such sluggishness is to be expected in my untried condition. I detect no unmistakable indications of enemy trickery, but I am still uneasy. Impatiently I await the orders of my commander.

12

"I don't care what you do, Jimmy—just do *something*! Ah, of course I don't mean that literally. Of course I care. The well-being of the citizens of Cold City is, after all, my chief concern. What I mean is, I'm giving you carte blanche—full powers. You must act at once, Jimmy. Before the sun sets I want to see your evacuation plan on my desk for signature."

"Surely, Mr. Mayor, I understand. But what am I supposed to work with? I have no transport yet. The Army has promised a fleet of D-100 tractors pulling 100x cargo flats, but none have materialized. They were caught just as short as we were, Your Honor, even though that General Bates knew all about it. We all knew the day would come, but I guess we kept hoping 'maybe.' Our negotiations with them seemed to be bearing fruit, and the idea of exposing over a million and a half city-bred individuals to a twelve-hundred-mile trek in thirty-below temperatures was just too awful to really face. Even now—"

"I know. The Army is doing all it can. The main body of PR troops hasn't actually crossed the dateline yet—so perhaps our forces can get in position. Who knows? Miracles have happened before. But we can't base our thinking on miracles, Jimmy. Flats or no flats, we have to have the people out of the dome before enemy forces cut us off."

"Mr. Mayor, our people can't take this. Aside from leaving their homes and possessions—I've already started them packing, and I've given them a ten-pounds-per-person limit—they aren't used to exercise, to say nothing of walking twelve hundred miles over frozen tundra. And most of them have no clothing heavier than a business suit. And—"

"Enough, Jimmy. I was ambushed in my office earlier today by an entire family: the old grandmother who was born under the dome and refused to consider going outside; the father all full of his product-promotion plans and the new garden he'd just laid out; mother, complaining about junior having a cold and no warm clothes; and the kids, just waiting trustfully until the excitement was over and they could go home and be tucked into their warm beds with a tummyful of dinner. Ye gods, Jimmy! Can you imagine them after three weeks on the trail?"

13

"Just lean across the desk, fellows. Come on, gather round. Take a close look at the shoulder tab. Four stars—see 'em? Then go over to the Slab and do the same with General Margrave. You'll count six. It's as easy as that, boys. The General says no test. Sure, I told him the whole plan. His eyes just kept boring in. Even making contingency plans for deploying an untested and non-High-Command-approved weapon system is grounds for court-martial. He didn't say that; maybe I'm telepathic. In summary, the General says no."

14

I don't know, now. What I heard, even with everything we got on the line, dug in and ready for anything, they's still a ten-mile-wide gap the Peepreps can waltz through without getting even a dirty look. So if General Bates—oh, he's a nice enough young fellow, after you get used to him—if he wants to plug the hole with old unit DNE here, why, I say go to it, only the Council says nix. I can say this much: she's put together so she'll stay together. I must of wired in a thousand of them damage-sensors myself, and that ain't a spot on what's on the diagram. "Pain circuits," old Doc Chin calls 'em. Says it's just like a instinct for self-preservation or something, like people. Old Denny can hurt, he says, so he'll be all the better at dodging enemy fire. He can enjoy, too, Doc says. He gets a kick out of doing his job right, and out of learning stuff. And he learns fast. He'll do okay against them: durn Peepreps. They got him programmed right to the brim with everything from them Greeks used to fight with no pants down to Avery's Last Stand at Leadpipe. He ain't no dumb private; he's got more dope to work on than any general ever graduated from the Point. And he's got more firepower than an old-time army corps. So I think maybe General Bates got aholt of a good idear there, myself. Says he can put her in the gap in his line and field-test her for fair, with the whole durn Peeprep army and air force for a test problem. Save the gubment some money, too. I heard Doc Chin say the full-scale field-test mock-up would run GM a hundred million and another five times that in army R-and-D funds. He had a map showed where he could use Denny here to block off the south end of Grand Crevasse where the Peeprep armor will have to travel 'count of the rugged terrain north of Cold City, and bottle 'em up slick as a owl's peter. I'm for it, durn it. Let Denny have his chance. Can't be no worse'n having them Comrades down here running things even worse'n the gubment.

15

"You don't understand, young man. My goodness, I'm not the least bit interested in bucking the line, as you put it. Heavens, I'm going back to my apartment—"

"I'm sorry, ma'am. I got my orders. This here ain't no drill; you got to keep it closed up. They're loading as fast as they can. It's my job to keep these lines moving right out the lock, so they get that flat loaded and get the next one up. We got over a million people to load by six AM deadline. So you just be nice, ma'am, and think about all the trouble it'd make if everybody decided to start back upstream and jam the elevators and all."

16

Beats me. 'Course, the good part about being just a hired man is I got no big decisions to make, so I don't hafta know what's going on. Seems like they'd let me know something, though. Batesey was down again, spent a hour with old Denny—like I say, beats me—but he give me a new data-can to program into her, right in her Action/Command section. Something's up. I just fired a N-class pulse at old Denny (them's the closest to the real thing) and she snapped her aft-quarter battery around so fast I couldn't see it move. Old Denny's keyed up, I know that much.

17

This has been a memorable time for me. I have my assignment at last, and I have conferred at length—for 2.037 seconds—with my Commander. I am now a fighting unit of the 20th Virginia, a regiment ancient and honorable, with a history dating back to Terra Insula. I look forward to my opportunity to demonstrate my worthiness.

18

"I assure you, gentlemen, the rumor in unfounded. I have by no means authorized the deployment of 'an untested and potentially highly dangerous machine,' as your memo termed it. Candidly, I was not at first entirely unsympathetic to the proposal of the Chief of Ground Forces, in view of the circumstances—I presume you're aware that the PR committed its forces to invasion over an hour ago, and that they are advancing in overwhelming strength. I have issued the order to commence the evacuation, and I believe that the initial phases are even now in progress. I have the fullest confidence in General Bates and can assure you that our forces will do all in their power in the face of this dastardly sneak attack. As for the unfortunate publicity given to the earlier suggestion re the use of the Mark XX, I can tell you that I at once subjected the data to computer analysis here at Headquarters to determine whether any potentially useful purpose could be served by risking the use of the new machine without prior test certification. The results were negative. I'm sorry, gentlemen, but that's it. The enemy has the advantage both strategically and tactically. We are outgunned, outmanned, and in effect outflanked. There is nothing we can do save attempt to hold them long enough to permit the evacuation to get underway, then retreat in good order. The use of our orbiting nuclear capability is out of the question. It is, after all, our own territory we'd be devastating. No more questions for the present, please, gentlemen. I have my duties to see to."

19

My own situation continues to deteriorate. The Current Status program has been updated to within 21 seconds of the present. The reasons both for what is normally a pre-engagement updating and for the hiatus of 21 seconds remain obscure. However, I shall of course hold myself in readiness for whatever comes.

20

"It's all nonsense: to call me here at this hour merely to stand by and watch the destruction of our gallant men who are giving their lives in a totally hopeless fight against overwhelming odds. We know what the outcome must be. You yourself, General, informed us this afternoon that the big tactical computer has analyzed the situation and reported no possibility of stopping them with what we've got. By the way, did you include the alternative of use of the big, er, Bolo, I believe they're called—frightening things—they're so damned *big!* But if, in desperation, you should be forced to employ the thing— have you that result as well? I see. No hope at all. So there's nothing we can do. This is a sad day, General. But I fail to see what object is served by getting me out of bed to come down here. Not that I'm not willing to do anything I can, of course. With our people—innocent civilians—out on that blizzard-swept tundra tonight, and our boys dying to gain them a little time, the loss of a night's sleep is relatively unimportant, of course. But it's my duty to be at my best, rested and ready to face the decisions that we of the Council will be called on to make.

"Now, General, kindly excuse my ignorance if I don't understand all this … but I understood that the large screen there was placed so as to monitor the action at the southern debouchment of Grand Crevasse where we expect the enemy armor to emerge to make its dash for Cold City and the Complex. Yes, indeed, so I was saying, but in that case I'm afraid I don't understand. I'm quite sure you stated that the untried Mark XX would *not* be used. Yet on the screen I see what appears to be in fact that very machine moving up. Please, *calmly,* General! I quite understand your position. Defiance of a direct order? That's rather serious, I'm sure, but no occasion for such language, General. There must be some explanation."

21

This is a most satisfying development. Quite abruptly my Introspection Complex was brought up to full operating level, extra power resources were made available to my Current-Action memory stage, and most satisfying of all, my Battle Reflex circuit has been activated at Active Service level. Action is impending, I am sure of it. It is a curious anomaly: I dread the prospect of damage and even possible destruction, but even more strongly I anticipate the pleasure of performing my design function.

22

"Yes, sir, I agree. It's mutiny. But I will not recall the Bolo and I will not report myself under arrest. Not until this battle's over, General. So the hell with my career. I've got a war to win."

23

"Now just let me get this quite straight, General. Having been denied authority to field-test this new device, you—or a subordinate, which amounts to the same thing—have placed the machine in the line of battle, in open defiance of the Council. This is a serious matter, General. Yes, of course it's war, but to attempt to defend your actions now will merely exacerbate the matter. In any event—to return to your curious decision to defy Council authority and to reverse your own earlier position—it was yourself who assured me that no useful purpose could be served by fielding this experimental equipment; that the battle, and perhaps the war, and the very self-determination of West Continent are irretrievably lost. There is nothing we can do save accept the situation gracefully while decrying Chairman Smith's decision to resort to force. Yes indeed, General, I should like to observe on the Main Tactical Display screen. Shall we go along?"

24

"Now, there at center screen, Mr. Counselor, you see that big blue rectangular formation. Actually that's the opening of Grand Crevasse, emerges through an ice tunnel, you know. Understand the Crevasse is a crustal fault, a part of the same formation that created the thermal sink from which the Complex draws its energy. Splendid spot for an ambush, of course, if we had the capability. Enemy has little option; like a highway in there—armor can move up at flank speed. Above, the badlands, where *we* must operate. Now, over to the left, you see that smoke, or dust or whatever. That represents the western limit of the unavoidable gap in General Bates's line. Dust raised by maneuvering Mark XVs, you understand. Obsolete equipment, but we'll do what we can with them. Over to the right, in the distance there, we can make out our forward artillery emplacement of the Threshold Line. Pitiful, really. Yes, Mr. Counselor, there is indeed a gap precisely opposite the point where the lead units of the enemy are expected to appear. Clearly anything in their direct line of advance will be annihilated; thus General Bates has wisely chosen to dispose his forces to cover both enemy flanks, putting him in position to counterattack if opportunity offers. We must, after all, sir, use what we have. Theoretical arms programmed for fiscal ninety are of no use whatever today. Umm. As for that, one must be flexible, modifying plans to meet a shifting tactical situation. Faced with the prospect of seeing the enemy drive through our center and descend unopposed on the vital installations at Cold City, I have, as you see, decided to order General Bates to make use of the experimental Mark XX. Certainly—my decision entirely. I take full responsibility."

25

I advance over broken terrain toward my assigned position. The prospect of action exhilarates me, but my assessment of enemy strength indicates they are fielding approximately 17.4 percent greater weight of armor than anticipated, with commensurately greater firepower. I compute that I am grossly overmatched. Nonetheless, I shall do my best.

26

"There's no doubt whatever, gentlemen. Computers work with hard facts. Given the enemy's known offensive capability and our own defensive resources, it's a simple computation. No combination of the manpower and equipment at our command can possibly inflict a defeat on the PR forces at this time and place. Two is greater than one. You can't make a dollar out of fifteen cents."

27

"At least we can gather some useful data from the situation, gentlemen. The Bolo Mark XX has been committed to battle. Its designers assure me that the new self-motivating circuitry will vastly enhance the combat-effectiveness of the Bolo. Let us observe."

28

Hate to see old Denny out there, just a great big sitting duck, all alone and—here they come! Look at 'em boiling out of there like ants out of a hot log. Can't hardly look at that screen, them tactical nukes popping fireworks all over the place. But old Denny know enough to get under cover. See that kind of glow all around him? All right, *it,* then. You know, working with him—it—so long, it got to feeling almost like he was somebody. Sure, I know, anyway, that's vaporized ablative shield you see. They're making it plenty hot for him. But he's fighting back. Them Hellbores is putting out, and they know it. Looks like they're concentrating on him now. Look at them tracers closing in on him! Come on, Denny, you ain't dumb. Get out of there fast.

29

"Certainly it's aware what's at stake! I've told you he—the machine, that is—has been fully programmed and is well aware not only of the tactical situation but of strategic and logistical considerations as well. Certainly it's an important item of equipment; its loss would be a serious blow to our present underequipped forces. You may rest assured that its pain circuits as well as its basic military competence will cause it to take the proper action. The fact that I originally opposed commissioning the device is not to be taken as implying any lack of confidence on my part in its combat-effectiveness. You may consider that my reputation is staked on the performance of the machine. It will act correctly."

30

It appears that the Enemy is absorbing my barrage with little effect. More precisely, for each Enemy unit destroyed by my fire 2.4 fresh units immediately move out to replace it. Thus it appears I am ineffective, while already my own shielding is suffering severe damage. Yet while I have offensive capability I must carry on as my commander would wish.

The pain is very great now, but thanks to my superb circuitry I am not disabled, though it has been necessary to withdraw my power from my external somatic sensors.

31

"I can assure you, gentlemen, insofar as simple logic functions are concerned, the Mark XX is perfectly capable of assessing the situation even as you and I, only better. Doubtless as soon as it senses that its position has grown totally untenable, it will retreat to the shelter of the rock ridge and retire under cover to a position from which it can return fire without taking the full force of the enemy's attack at point-blank range. It's been fully briefed on late developments, it knows this is a hopeless fight. There, you see? It's moving ...."

32

"I thought you said—dammit, I *know* you said your pet machine had brains enough to know when to pull out! But look at it: half a billion plus of Concordiat funds being bombarded into radioactive rubbish. Like shooting fish in a barrel."

33

"Yes, sir, I'm monitoring everything. My test panel is tuned to it across the board. I'm getting continuous reading on all still-active circuits. Battle Reflex is still hot. Pain circuits close to overload, but he's still taking it. I don't know how much more he can take, sir; already way past redline. Expected him to break off and get out before now."

34

"It's a simple matter of arithmetic; there is only one correct course of action in any given military situation. The big tactical computer was designed specifically to compare data and deduce that sole correct action. In this case my readout shows that the only thing the Mark XX could legitimately do at this point is just what the Professor here says: pull back to cover and continue its barrage. The onboard computing capability of the unit is as capable of reaching that conclusion, as is the big computer at HQ. So keep calm, gentlemen. It will withdraw at any moment, I assure you of that."

35

"Now it's getting ready—no, look what it's doing! It's advancing into the teeth of that murderous fire. By God, you've got to admire that workmanship! That it's still capable of moving is a miracle. All the ablative metal is gone—you can see its bare armor exposed—and it takes some heat to make that flint-steel glow white!"

36

"Certainly, I'm looking. I see it. By God, sir, it's still moving—faster, in fact! Charging the enemy line like the Light Brigade! And all for nothing, it appears. Your machine, General, appears less competent than you expected."

37

Poor old Denny. Made his play and played out, I reckon. Readings on the board over there don't look good; durn near every overload in him blowed wide open. Not much there to salvage. Emergency Survival Center's hot. Never expected to see *that*. Means all kinds of breakdowns inside. But it figures, after what he just went through. Look at that slag pit he drove up out of. They wanted a field test. Reckon they got it. And he flunked it.

38

"Violating orders and winning is one thing, George. Committing mutiny and losing is quite another. Your damned machine made a fool of me. After I stepped in and backed you to the hilt and stood there like a jackass and assured Councillor Grace that the thing knew what it was doing—it blows the whole show. Instead of pulling back to save itself it charged to destruction. I want an explanation of this fiasco at once."

39

"Look! No, by God, over *there!* On the left of the entrance. They're breaking formation—they're running for it! Watch this! The whole spearhead is crumbling, they're taking to the badlands, they're—"

40

"*Why*, dammit? It's outside all rationality. As far as the enemy's concerned, fine. They broke and ran. They couldn't stand up to the sight of the Mark XX not only taking everything they had, but advancing on them out of that inferno, all guns blazing. Another hundred yards and—but they don't know that. It buffaloed them, so score a battle won for our side. But *why?* I'd stack my circuits up against any fixed installation in existence, including the big Tacomp the Army's so proud of. That machine was as aware as anybody that the only smart thing to do was run. So now I've got a junk pile on my hands. Some test! A clear flunk. Destroyed in action. Not recommended for Federal procurement. Nothing left but a few hot transistors in the Survival Center. It's a disaster, Fred. All my work, all your work, the whole program wrecked. Fred, you talk to General Bates. As soon as he's done inspecting the hulk he'll want somebody human to chew out."

41

"Look at that pile of junk! Reading off the scale. Won't be cool enough to haul to Disposal for six months. I understand you're Chief Engineer at Bolo Division. You built this thing. Maybe you can tell me what you had in mind here. Sure, it stood up to fire better than I hoped. But so what? A stone wall can stand and take it. This thing is supposed to be *smart*, supposed to feel pain like a living creature. Blunting the strike at the Complex was a valuable contribution, but how can I recommend procurement of this junk heap?"

42

Why, Denny? Just tell me why you did it. You got all these military brass down on you, and on me, too. On all of us. They don't much like stuff they can't understand. You attacked when they figured you to run. Sure, you routed the enemy, like Bates says, but you got yourself ruined in the process. Don't make sense. Any dumb private, along with the generals, would have known enough to get out of there. Tell me why, so I'll have something for Bates to put on his Test Evaluation Report, AGF Form 1103-6, Rev 11/3/85.

43

"All right, Unit DNE of the line. Why did you do it? This is your Commander, Unit DNE. Report! Why did you do it? Now, you knew your position was hopeless, didn't you? That you'd be destroyed if you held your ground, to say nothing of advancing. Surely you were able to compute that. You were lucky to have the chance to prove yourself."

For a minute I thought old Denny was too far gone to answer. There was just a kind of groan come out of the amplifier. Then it firmed up. General Bates had his hand cupped behind his ear, but Denny spoke right up.

"*Yes, sir.*"

"You knew what was at stake here. It was the ultimate test of your ability to perform correctly under stress, of your suitability as a weapon of war. You knew that. General Margrave and old Priss Grace and the press boys all had their eyes on every move you made. So instead of using common sense, you waded into that inferno in defiance of all logic—and destroyed yourself. Right?"

"*That is correct, sir.*"

"Then why? In the name of sanity, tell me *why*! Why, instead of backing out and saving yourself, did you charge? ... Wait a minute, Unit DNE. It just dawned on me. I've been underestimating you. You *knew,* didn't you? Your knowledge of human psychology told you they'd break and run, didn't it?"

"No, sir. On the contrary, I was quite certain that they were as aware as I that they held every advantage."

"Then that leaves me back where I started. Why? What made you risk everything on a hopeless attack? Why did you do it?"

"For the honor of the regiment."

The Last Command

I come to *awareness, sensing a residual oscillation traversing me from an arbitrarily designated heading of 035. From the damping rate I compute that the shock was of intensity 8.7, emanating from a source within the limits 72 meters/46 meters. I activate my primary screens, trigger a return salvo. There is no response. I engage reserve energy cells, bring my secondary battery to bear—futilely. It is apparent that I have been ranged by the Enemy and severely damaged.*

My positional sensors indicate that I am resting at an angle of 13 degrees 14 seconds, deflected from a baseline at 21 points from median. I attempt to right myself, but encounter massive resistance. I activate my forward scanners, shunt power to my I-R microstrobes. Not a flicker illuminates my surroundings. I am encased in utter blackness.

Now a secondary shock wave approaches, rocks me with an intensity of 8.2. It is apparent that I must withdraw from my position—but my drive trains remain inert under full thrust. I shift to base emergency power, try again. Pressure mounts; I sense my awareness fading under the intolerable strain; then, abruptly, resistance falls off and I am in motion.

It is not the swift maneuvering of full drive, however; I inch forward, as if restrained by massive barriers. Again I attempt to penetrate the surrounding darkness and this time perceive great irregular outlines shot through with fracture planes. I probe cautiously, then more vigorously, encountering incredible densities.

I channel all available power to a single ranging pulse, direct it upward. The indication is so at variance with all experience that I repeat the test at a new angle. Now I must accept the fact: I am buried under 207.6 meters of solid rock!

I direct my attention to an effort to orient myself to my uniquely desperate situation. I run through an action-status checklist of thirty thousand items, feel dismay at the extent of power loss. My main cells are almost completely drained, my reserve units at no more than .4 charge. Thus my sluggishness is explained. I review the tactical situation, recall the triumphant announcement from my commander that the Enemy forces were annihilated, that all resistance had ceased. In memory, I review the formal procession; in company with my comrades of the Dinochrome Brigade, many of us deeply scarred by Enemy action, we parade before the Grand Commandant, then assemble on the depot ramp. At command, we bring our music storage cells into phase and display our Battle Anthem. The nearby star radiates over a full spectrum unfiltered by atmospheric haze. It is a moment of glorious triumph. Then the final command is given—

The rest is darkness. But it is apparent that the victory celebration was premature. The Enemy has counterattacked with a force that has come near to immobilizing me. The realization is shocking, but the .1 second of leisurely introspection has clarified my position. At once, I broadcast a call on Brigade Action wavelength:

"Unit LNE to Command, requesting permission to file VSR."

I wait, sense no response, call again, using full power. I sweep the enclosing volume of rock with an emergency alert warning. I tune to the all-units band, await the replies of my comrades of the Brigade. None answer. Now I must face the reality: I alone have survived the assault.

I channel my remaining power to my drive and detect a channel of reduced density. I press for it and the broken rock around me yields reluctantly. Slowly, I move forward and upward. My pain circuitry shocks my awareness center with emergency signals; I am doing irreparable damage to my overloaded neural systems, but my duty is clear: I must seek out and engage the Enemy.

2

Emerging from behind the blast barrier, Chief Engineer Pete Reynolds of the New Devonshire Port Authority pulled off his rock mask and spat grit from his mouth.

"That's the last one; we've bottomed out at just over two hundred yards. Must have hit a hard stratum down there."

"It's almost sundown," the paunchy man beside him said shortly. "You're a day and a half behind schedule."

"We'll start backfilling now, Mr. Mayor. I'll have pilings poured by oh-nine hundred tomorrow, and with any luck the first section of pad will be in place in time for the rally."

"I'm—" The mayor broke off, looked startled. "I thought you told me that was the last charge to be fired …."

Reynolds frowned. A small but distinct tremor had shaken the ground underfoot. A few feet away, a small pebble balanced atop another toppled and fell with a faint clatter.

"Probably a big rock fragment falling," he said. At that moment, a second vibration shook the earth, stronger this time. Reynolds heard a rumble and a distant impact as rock fell from the side of the newly blasted excavation. He whirled to the control shed as the door swung back and Second Engineer Mayfield appeared.

"Take a look at this, Pete!"

Reynolds went across to the hut, stepped inside. Mayfield was bending over the profiling table.

"What do you make of it?" he pointed. Superimposed on the heavy red contour representing the detonation of the shaped charge that had completed the drilling of the final pile core were two other traces, weak but distinct.

"About .1 intensity." Mayfield looked puzzled. "What—"

The tracking needle dipped suddenly, swept up the screen to peak at .21, dropped back. The hut trembled. A stylus fell from the edge of the table. The red face of Mayor Dougherty burst through the door.

"Reynolds, have you lost your mind? What's the idea of blasting while I'm standing out in the open? I might have been killed!"

"I'm not blasting," Reynolds snapped. "Jim, get Eaton on the line, see if they know anything." He stepped to the door, shouted. A heavyset man in sweat-darkened coveralls swung down from the seat of a cable-lift rig.

"Boss, what goes on?" he called as he came up. "Damn near shook me out of my seat!"

"I don't know. You haven't set any trim charges?"

"Jesus, no, boss. I wouldn't set no charges without your say-so."

"Come on." Reynolds started out across the rubble-littered stretch of barren ground selected by the Authority as the site of the new spaceport. Halfway to the open mouth of the newly blasted pit, the ground under his feet rocked violently enough to make him stumble. A gout of dust rose from the excavation ahead. Loose rock danced on the ground. Beside him the drilling chief grabbed his arm.

"Boss, we better get back!"

Reynolds shook him off, kept going. The drill chief swore and followed. The shaking of the ground went on, a sharp series of thumps interrupting a steady trembling.

"It's a quake!" Reynolds yelled over the low rumbling sound.

He and the chief were at the rim of the core now.

"It can't be a quake, boss," the latter shouted. "Not in these formations!"

"Tell it to the geologists—" The rock slab they were standing on rose a foot, dropped back. Both men fell. The slab bucked like a small boat in choppy water.

"Let's get out of here!" Reynolds was up and running. Ahead, a fissure opened, gaped a foot wide. He jumped it, caught a glimpse of black depths, a glint of wet clay twenty feet below—

A hoarse scream stopped him in his tracks. He spun, saw the drill chief down, a heavy splinter of rock across his legs. He jumped to him, heaved at the rock. There was blood on the man's shirt. The chief's hands beat the dusty rock before him. Then other men were there, grunting, sweaty hands gripping beside Reynolds. The ground rocked. The roar from under the earth had risen to a deep, steady rumble. They lifted the rock aside, picked up the injured man, and stumbled with him to the aid shack.

The mayor was there, white-faced.

"What is it, Reynolds? By God, if you're responsible—"

"Shut up!" Reynolds brushed him aside, grabbed the phone, punched keys.

"Eaton! What have you got on this temblor?"

"Temblor, hell." The small face on the four-inch screen looked like a ruffled hen. "What in the name of Order are you doing out there? I'm reading a whole series of displacements originating from that last core of yours! What did you do, leave a pile of trim charges lying around?"

"It's a quake. Trim charges, hell! This thing's broken up two hundred yards of surface rock. It seems to be traveling north-northeast—"

"I see that; a traveling earthquake!" Eaton flapped his arms, a tiny and ridiculous figure against a background of wall charts and framed diplomas. "Well—do something, Reynolds! Where's Mayor Dougherty?"

"Underfoot!" Reynolds snapped, and cut off.

Outside, a layer of sunset-stained dust obscured the sweep of level plain. A rock-dozer rumbled up, ground to a halt by Reynolds. A man jumped down.

"I got the boys moving equipment out," he panted. "The thing's cutting a trail straight as a rule for the highway!" He pointed to a raised roadbed a quarter mile away.

"How fast is it moving?"

"She's done a hundred yards; it hasn't been ten minutes yet!"

"If it keeps up another twenty minutes, it'll be into the Intermix!"

"Scratch a few million cees and six months' work then, Pete!"

"And Southside Mall's a couple miles farther."

"Hell, it'll damp out before then!"

"Maybe. Grab a field car, Dan."

"Pete!" Mayfield came up at a trot. "This thing's building! The centroid's moving on a heading of oh-two-two—"

"How far subsurface?"

"It's rising; started at two-twenty yards, and it's up to one-eighty!"

"What the hell have we stirred up?" Reynolds stared at Mayfield as the field car skidded to a stop beside them.

"Stay with it, Jim. Give me anything new. We're taking a closer look." He climbed into the rugged vehicle.

"Take a blast truck—"

"No time!" He waved and the car gunned away into the pall of dust.

3

The rock car pulled to a stop at the crest of the three-level Intermix on a lay-by designed to permit tourists to enjoy the view of the site of the proposed port, a hundred feet below. Reynolds studied the progress of the quake through field glasses. From this vantage point, the path of the phenomenon was a clearly defined trail of tilted and broken rock, some of the slabs twenty feet across. As he watched, the fissure lengthened.

"It looks like a mole's trail." Reynolds handed the glasses to his companion, thumbed the send key on the car radio.

"Jim, get Eaton and tell him to divert all traffic from the Circular south of Zone Nine. Cars are already clogging the right-of-way. The dust is visible from a mile away, and when the word gets out there's something going on, we'll be swamped."

"I'll tell him, but he won't like it!"

"This isn't politics! This thing will be into the outer pad area in another twenty minutes!"

"It won't last—"

"How deep does it read now?"

"One-five!" There was a moment's silence. "Pete, if it stays on course, it'll surface at about where you're parked!"

"Uh-huh. It looks like you can scratch one Intermix. Better tell Eaton to get a story ready for the press."

"Pete, talking about newshounds—" Dan said beside him. Reynolds switched off, turned to see a man in a gay-colored driving outfit coming across from a battered Monojag sportster which had pulled up behind the rock car. A big camera case was slung across his shoulder.

"Say, what's going on down there?" he called.

"Rock slide," Reynolds said shortly. "I'll have to ask you to drive on. The road's closed to all traffic—"

"Who're you?" The man looked belligerent.

"I'm the engineer in charge. Now pull out, brother." He turned back to the radio. "Jim, get every piece of heavy equipment we own over here, on the double." He paused, feeling a minute trembling in the car. "The Intermix is beginning to feel it," he went on. "I'm afraid we're in for it. Whatever that thing is, it acts like a solid body boring its way through the ground. Maybe we can barricade it."

"Barricade an earthquake?"

"Yeah, I know how it sounds—but it's the only idea I've got."

"Hey—what's that about an earthquake?" The man in the colored suit was still there. "By gosh, I can feel it—the whole damned bridge is shaking!"

"Off, mister—now!" Reynolds jerked a thumb at the traffic lanes where a steady stream of cars were hurtling past. "Dan, take us over to the main track. We'll have to warn this traffic off—"

"Hold on, fellow." The man unlimbered his camera. "I represent the New Devon *Scope*. I have a few questions—"

"I don't have the answers." Pete cut him off as the car pulled away.

"Hah!" The man who had questioned Reynolds yelled after him. "Big shot! Think you can ..." His voice was lost behind them.

4

In a modest retirees' apartment block in the coast town of Idlebreeze, forty miles from the scene of the freak quake, an old man sat in a reclining chair, half dozing before a yammering Tri-D tank.

"... Grandpa," a sharp-voiced young woman was saying. "It's time for you to go in to bed."

"Bed? Why do I want to go to bed? Can't sleep anyway ...." He stirred, made a pretense of sitting up, showing an interest in the Tri-D. "I'm watching this show. Don't bother me."

"It's not a show, it's the news," a fattish boy said disgustedly. "Ma, can I switch channels—"

"Leave it alone, Bennie," the old man said. On the screen a panoramic scene spread out, a stretch of barren ground across which a furrow showed. As he watched, it lengthened.

"... up here at the Intermix we have a fine view of the whole curious business, lazangemmun," the announcer chattered. "And in our opinion it's some sort of publicity stunt staged by the Port Authority to publicize their controversial port project—"

"Ma, can I change channels?"

"Go ahead, Bennie—"

"Don't touch it," the old man said. The fattish boy reached for the control, but something in the old man's eye stopped him ....

5

"The traffic's still piling in here," Reynolds said into the phone. "Damn it, Jim, we'll have a major jam on our hands—"

"He won't do it, Pete! You know the Circular was his baby—the super all-weather pike that nothing could shut down. He says you'll have to handle this in the field—"

"Handle, hell! I'm talking about preventing a major disaster! And in a matter of minutes, at that!"

"I'll try again—"

"If he says no, divert a couple of the big ten-yard graders and block it off yourself. Set up field arcs, and keep any cars from getting in from either direction."

"Pete, that's outside your authority!"

"You heard me!"

Ten minutes later, back at ground level, Reynolds watched the boom-mounted polyarcs swinging into position at the two roadblocks a quarter of a mile apart, cutting off the threatened section of the raised expressway. A hundred yards from where he stood on the rear cargo deck of a light grader rig, a section of rock fifty feet wide rose slowly, split, fell back with a ponderous impact. One corner of it struck the massive pier supporting the extended shelf of the lay-by above. A twenty-foot splinter fell away, exposing the reinforcing-rod core.

"How deep, Jim?" Reynolds spoke over the roaring sound coming from the disturbed area.

"Just subsurface now, Pete! It ought to break through—" His voice was drowned in a rumble as the damaged pier shivered, rose up, buckled at its midpoint, and collapsed, bringing down with it a large chunk of pavement and guardrail, and a single still-glowing light pole. A small car that had been parked on the doomed section was visible for an instant just before the immense slab struck. Reynolds saw it bounce aside, then disappear under an avalanche of broken concrete.

"My God, Pete—" Dan started. "That damned fool newshound …!"

"Look!" As the two men watched, a second pier swayed, fell backward into the shadow of the span above. The roadway sagged, and two more piers snapped. With a bellow like a burst dam, a hundred-foot stretch of the road fell into the roiling dust cloud.

"Pete!" Mayfield's voice burst from the car radio. "Get out of there! I threw a reader on that thing and it's chattering off the scale …!"

Among the piled fragments something stirred, heaved, rising up, lifting multi-ton pieces of the broken road, thrusting them aside like so many potato chips. A dull blue radiance broke through from the broached earth, threw an eerie light on the shattered structure above. A massive, ponderously irresistible shape thrust forward through the ruins. Reynolds saw a great blue-glowing profile emerge from the rubble like a surfacing submarine, shedding a burden of broken stone, saw immense treads ten feet wide claw for purchase, saw the mighty flank brush a still-standing pier, send it crashing aside.

"Pete, what—what is it …?"

"I don't know." Reynolds broke the paralysis that had gripped him. "Get us out of here, Dan, fast! Whatever it is, it's headed straight for the city!"

6

I emerge at last from the trap into which I had fallen, and at once encounter defensive words of considerable strength. My scanners are dulled from lack of power, but I am able to perceive open ground beyond the barrier, and farther still, at a distance of 5.7 kilometers, massive walls. Once more I transmit the Brigade Rally signal; but as before, there is no reply. I am truly alone.

I scan the surrounding area for the emanations of Enemy drive units, monitor the EM spectrum for their communications. I detect nothing; either my circuitry is badly damaged, or their shielding is superb.

I must now make a decision as to possible courses of action. Since all my comrades of the Brigade have fallen, I compute that the fortress before me must be held by Enemy forces. I direct probing signals at them, discover them to be of unfamiliar construction, and less formidable than they appear. I am aware of the possibility that this may be a trick of the Enemy; but my course is clear.

I reengage my driving engines and advance on the Enemy fortress.

7

"You're out of your mind, father," the stout man said. "At your age—"

"At your age, I got my nose smashed in a brawl in a bar on Aldo," the old man cut him off. "But I won the fight."

"James, you can't go out at this time of night …" an elderly woman wailed.

"Tell them to go home." The old man walked painfully toward his bedroom door. "I've seen enough of them for today." He passed out of sight.

"Mother, you won't let him do anything foolish?"

"He'll forget about it in a few minutes; but maybe you'd better go now and let him settle down."

"Mother—I really think a home is the best solution."

"Yes," the young woman nodded agreement. "After all, he's past ninety—and he has his veteran's retirement …."

Inside his room, the old man listened as they departed. He went to the closet, took out clothes, began dressing ….

8

City Engineer Eaton's face was chalk-white on the screen.

"No one can blame me," he said. "How could I have known—"

"Your office ran the surveys and gave the PA the green light," Mayor Dougherty yelled.

"All the old survey charts showed was 'Disposal Area,'" Eaton threw out his hands. "I assumed—"

"As City Engineer, you're not paid to make assumptions! Ten minutes' research would have told you that was a 'Y' category area!"

"What's 'Y' category mean?" Mayfield asked Reynolds. They were standing by the field comm center, listening to the dispute. Nearby, boom-mounted Tri-D cameras hummed, recording the progress of the immense machine, its upper turret rearing forty-five feet into the air, as it ground slowly forward across smooth ground toward the city, dragging behind it a trailing festoon of twisted reinforcing iron crusted with broken concrete.

"Half-life over one hundred years," Reynolds answered shortly. "The last skirmish of the war was fought near here. Apparently this is where they buried the radioactive equipment left over from the battle."

"But what the hell, that was seventy years ago—"

"There's still enough residual radiation to contaminate anything inside a quarter-mile radius."

"They must have used some hellish stuff." Mayfield stared at the dull shine half a mile distant.

"Reynolds, how are you going to stop this thing?" The mayor had turned on the PA engineer.

"Me stop it? You saw what it did to my heaviest rigs: flattened them like pancakes. You'll have to call out the military on this one, Mr. Mayor."

"Call in Federation forces? Have them meddling in civic affairs?"

"The station's only sixty-five miles from here. I think you'd better call them fast. It's only moving at about three miles per hour but it will reach the south edge of the Mall in another forty-five minutes."

"Can't you mine it? Blast a trap in its path?"

"You saw it claw its way up from six hundred feet down. I checked the specs; it followed the old excavation tunnel out. It was rubble-filled and capped with twenty-inch compressed concrete."

"It's incredible," Eaton said from the screen. "The entire machine was encased in a ten-foot shell of reinforced armocrete. It had to break out of that before it could move a foot!"

"That was just a radiation shield; it wasn't intended to restrain a Bolo Combat Unit."

"What was, may I inquire?" The mayor glared from one face to another.

"The units were deactivated before being buried," Eaton spoke up, as if he were eager to talk. "Their circuits were fused. It's all in the report—"

"The report you should have read somewhat sooner," the mayor snapped.

"What—what started it up?" Mayfield looked bewildered. "For seventy years it was down there, and nothing happened!"

"Our blasting must have jarred something," Reynolds said shortly. "Maybe closed a relay that started up the old battle reflex circuit."

"You know something about these machines?" The mayor beetled his brows at him.

"I've read a little."

"Then speak up, man. I'll call the station, if you feel I must. What measures should I request?"

"I don't know, Mr. Mayor. As far as I know, nothing on New Devon can stop that machine now."

The mayor's mouth opened and closed. He whirled to the screen, blanked Eaton's agonized face, punched in the code for the Federation station.

"Colonel Blane!" he blurted as a stern face came onto the screen. "We have a major emergency on our hands! I'll need everything you've got! This is the situation ...."

9

I encounter no resistance other than the flimsy barrier, but my progress is slow. Grievous damage has been done to my main drive sector due to overload during my escape from the trap; and the failure of my sensing circuitry has deprived me of a major portion of my external receptivity. Now my pain circuits project a continuous signal to my awareness center, but it is my duty to my Commander and to my fallen comrades of the Brigade to press forward at my best speed; but my performance is a poor shadow of my former ability.

And now at last the Enemy comes into action! I sense aerial units closing at supersonic velocities; I lock my lateral batteries to them and direct salvo fire, but I sense that the arming mechanisms clatter harmlessly. The craft sweep over me, and my impotent guns elevate, track them as they release detonants that spread out in an envelopmental pattern which I, with my reduced capabilities, am powerless to avoid. The missiles strike; I sense their detonations all about me; but I suffer only trivial damage. The Enemy has blundered if he thought to neutralize a Mark XXVIII Combat Unit with mere chemical explosives! But I weaken with each meter gained.

Now there is no doubt as to my course. I must press the charge and carry the walls before my reserve cells are exhausted.

10

From a vantage point atop a bucket rig four hundred yards from the position the great fighting machine had now reached, Pete Reynolds studied it through night glasses. A battery of beamed polyarcs pinned the giant hulk, scarred and rust-scaled, in a pool of blue-white light. A mile and a half beyond it, the walls of the Mall rose sheer from the garden setting.

"The bombers slowed it some," he reported to Eaton via scope. "But it's still making better than two miles per hour. I'd say another twenty-five minutes before it hits the main ringwall. How's the evacuation going?"

"Badly! I get no cooperation! You'll be my witness, Reynolds, I did all I could—"

"How about the mobile batteries; how long before they'll be in position?" Reynolds cut him off.

"I've heard nothing from Federation Central—typical militaristic arrogance, not keeping me informed—but I have them on my screens. They're two miles out—say three minutes."

"I hope you made your point about N-heads."

"That's outside my province!" Eaton said sharply. "It's up to Brand to carry out this portion of the operation!"

"The HE Missiles didn't do much more than clear away the junk it was dragging." Reynolds' voice was sharp.

"I wash my hands of responsibility for civilian lives," Eaton was saying when Reynolds shut him off, changed channels.

"Jim, I'm going to try to divert it," he said crisply. "Eaton's sitting on his political fence; the Feds are bringing artillery up, but I don't expect much from it. Technically, Brand needs Sector okay to use nuclear stuff, and he's not the boy to stick his neck out—"

"Divert it how? Pete, don't take any chances—"

Reynolds laughed shortly. "I'm going to get around it and drop a shaped drilling charge in its path. Maybe I can knock a tread off. With luck, I might get its attention on me and draw it away from the Mall. There are still a few thousand people over there, glued to their Tri-D's. They think it's all a swell show."

"Pete, you can't walk up on that thing! It's hot—" He broke off. "Pete, there's some kind of nut here—he claims he has to talk to you; says he knows something about that damned juggernaut. Shall I ...?"

Reynolds paused with his hand on the cutoff switch. "Put him on," he snapped. Mayfield's face moved aside and an ancient, bleary-eyed visage stared out at him. The tip of the old man's tongue touched his dry lips.

"Son, I tried to tell this boy here, but he wouldn't listen—"

"What have you got, old timer?" Pete cut in. "Make it fast."

"My name's Sanders. James Sanders. I'm ... I was with the Planetary Volunteer Scouts, back in '71—"

"Sure, dad," Pete said gently. "I'm sorry, I've got a little errand to run—"

"Wait ...." The old man's face worked. "I'm old, son—too damned old. I know. But bear with me. I'll try to say it straight. I was with Hayle's squadron at Toledo. Then afterwards, they shipped us—but hell, you don't care about that! I keep wandering, son; can't help it. What I mean to say is—I was in on that last scrap, right here at New Devon—only we didn't call it New Devon then. Called it Heliport. Nothing but bare rock and Enemy emplacement ...."

"You were talking about the battle, Mr. Sanders," Pete said tensely. "Go on with that part."

"Lieutenant Sanders," the oldster said. "Sure, I was Acting Brigade Commander. See, our major was hit at Toledo—and after Tommy Chee stopped a sidewinder at Belgrave—"

"Stick to the point, Lieutenant!"

"Yessir!" The old man pulled himself together with an obvious effort. "I took the Brigade in; put out flankers, and ran the Enemy into the ground. We mopped 'em up in a thirty-three hour running fight that took us from over by Crater Bay all the way down here to Hellport. When it was over, I'd lost sixteen units, but the Enemy was done. They gave us Brigade Honors for that action. And then ..."

"Then what?"

"Then the triple-dyed yellow-bottoms at Headquarters put out the order the Brigade was to be scrapped; said they were too hot to make decon practical. Cost too much, they said! So after the final review—" he gulped, blinked—"they planted 'em deep, two hundred meters, and poured in special high-R concrete."

"And packed rubble in behind them," Reynolds finished for him. "All right, Lieutenant, I believe you! Now for the big one: What started that machine on a rampage?"

"Should have known they couldn't hold down a Bolo Mark XXVIII!" The old man's eyes lit up. "Take more than a few million tons of rock to stop Lenny when his battle board was lit!"

"Lenny?"

"That's my old command unit out there, son. I saw the markings on the Tri-D. Unit LNE of the Dinochrome Brigade!"

"Listen!" Reynolds snapped out. "Here's what I intend to try ...." He outlined his plan.

"Ha!" Sanders snorted. "It's a gutsy notion, mister, but Lenny won't give it a sneeze."

"You didn't come here to tell me we were licked," Reynolds cut in. "How about Brand's batteries?"

"Hell, son, Lenny stood up to point-blank Hellbore fire on Toledo, and—"

"Are you telling me there's nothing we can do?"

"What's that? No, son, that's not what I'm saying ...."

"Then what!"

"Just tell these johnnies to get out of my way, mister. I think I can handle him."

11

At the field comm hut, Pete Reynolds watched as the man who had been Lieutenant Sanders of the Volunteer Scouts pulled shiny black boots over his thin ankles and stood. The blouse and trousers of royal blue polyon hung on his spare frame like wash on a line. He grinned, a skull's grin.

"It doesn't fit like it used to; but Lenny will recognize it. It'll help. Now, if you've got that power pack ready ...."

Mayfield handed over the old-fashioned field instrument Sanders had brought in with him.

"It's operating, sir—but I've already tried everything I've got on that infernal machine; I didn't get a peep out of it."

Sanders winked at him. "Maybe I know a couple of tricks you boys haven't heard about." He slung the strap over his bony shoulder and turned to Reynolds.

"Guess we better get going, mister. He's getting close."

In the rock car, Sanders leaned close to Reynolds' ear. "Told you those Federal guns wouldn't scratch Lenny. They're wasting their time."

Reynolds pulled the car to a stop at the crest of the road, from which point he had a view of the sweep of ground leading across to the city's edge. Lights sparkled all across the towers of New Devon.

Close to the walls, the converging fire of the ranked batteries of infinite repeaters drove into the glowing bulk of the machine, which plowed on, undeterred. As he watched, the firing ceased.

"Now, let's get in there, before they get some other damn-fool scheme going," Sanders said.

The rock car crossed the rough ground, swung wide to come up on the Bolo from the left side. Behind the hastily rigged radiation cover, Reynolds watched the immense silhouette grow before him.

"I knew they were big," he said. "But to see one up close like this—" He pulled to a stop a hundred feet from the Bolo.

"Look at the side ports," Sanders said, his voice crisper now. "He's firing antipersonnel charges—only his plates are flat. If they weren't, we wouldn't have gotten within half a mile." He undipped the microphone and spoke into it:

"Unit LNE, break off action and retire to ten-mile line!"

Reynolds' head jerked around to stare at the old man. His voice had rung with vigor and authority as he spoke the command.

The Bolo ground slowly ahead. Sanders shook his head, tried again.

"No answer, like that fella said. He must be running on nothing but memories now ...." He reattached the microphone, and before Reynolds could put out a hand, had lifted the anti-R cover and stepped off on the ground.

"Sanders—get back in here!" Reynolds yelled.

"Never mind, son. I've got to get in close. Contact induction." He started toward the giant machine. Frantically, Reynolds started the car, slammed it into gear, pulled forward.

"Better stay back." Sanders' voice came from his field radio. "This close, that screening won't do you much good."

"Get in the car!" Reynolds roared. "That's hard radiation!"

"Sure; feels funny, like a sunburn, about an hour after you come in from the beach and start to think maybe you got a little too much." He laughed. "But I'll get to him ...."

Reynolds braked to a stop, watched the shrunken figure in the baggy uniform as it slogged forward, leaning as against a sleet storm.

12

"I'm up beside him." Sanders' voice came through faintly on the field radio. "I'm going to try to swing up on his side. Don't feel like trying to chase him any farther."

Through the glasses, Reynolds watched the small figure, dwarfed by the immense bulk of the fighting machine, as he tried, stumbled, tried again, swung up on the flange running across the rear quarter inside the churning bogie wheel.

"He's up," he reported. "Damned wonder the track didn't get him ...."

Clinging to the side of the machine, Sanders lay for a moment, bent forward across the flange. Then he pulled himself up, wormed his way forward to the base of the rear quarter turret, wedged himself against it. He unslung the communicator, removed a small black unit, clipped it to the armor; it clung, held by a magnet. He brought the microphone up to his face.

In the comm shack, Mayfield leaned toward the screen, his eyes squinted in tension. Across the field, Reynolds held the glasses fixed on the man lying across the flank of the Bolo. They waited ....

13

The walls are before me, and I ready myself for a final effort, but suddenly I am aware of trickle currents flowing over my outer surface. Is this some new trick of the Enemy? I tune to the wave energies, trace the source. They originate at a point in contact with my aft port armor. I sense modulation, match receptivity to a computed pattern. And I hear a voice:

"Unit LNE, break it off, Lenny. We're pulling back now, boy. This is Command to LNE; pull back to ten miles. If you read me, Lenny, swing to port and halt."

I am not fooled by the deception. The order appears correct, but the voice is not that of my Commander. Briefly I regret that I cannot spare energy to direct a neutralizing power flow at the device the Enemy has attached to me. I continue my charge.

"Unit LNE! Listen to me, boy; maybe you don't recognize my voice, but it's me. You see, boy—some time has passed. I've gotten old. My voice has changed some, maybe. But it's me! Make a port turn, Lenny. Make it now!"

I am tempted to respond to the trick, for something in the false command seems to awaken secondary circuits which I sense have been long stilled. But I must not be swayed by the cleverness of the Enemy. My sensing circuitry has faded further as my energy cells drain; but I know where the Enemy lies. I move forward, but I am filled with agony, and only the memory of my comrades drives me on.

"Lenny, answer me. Transmit on the old private band—the one we agreed on. Nobody but me knows it, remember?"

Thus the Enemy seeks to beguile me into diverting precious power. But I will not listen.

"Lenny—not much time left. Another minute and you'll be into the walls. People are going to die. Got to stop you, Lenny. Hot here. My God, I'm hot. Not breathing too well, now. I can feel it; cutting through me like knives. You took a load of Enemy power, Lenny; and now I'm getting my share. Answer me, Lenny. Over to you …."

It will require only a tiny allocation of power to activate a communication circuit. I realize that it is only an Enemy trick, but I compute that by pretending to be deceived, I may achieve some trivial advantage. I adjust circuitry accordingly and transmit:

"Unit LNE to Command. Contact with Enemy defensive line imminent. Request supporting fire!"

"Lenny … you can hear me! Good boy, Lenny! Now make a turn, to port. Walls … close …."

"Unit LNE to Command. Request positive identification; transmit code 685749."

"Lenny—I can't … don't have code blanks. But it's me …."

"In absence of recognition code, your transmission disregarded," I send. And now the walls loom high above me. There are many lights, but I see them only vaguely. I am nearly blind now.

"Lenny—less'n two hundred feet to go. Listen, Lenny. I'm climbing down. I'm going to jump down, Lenny, and get around under your fore scanner pickup. You'll see me, Lenny. You'll know me then."

The false transmission ceases. I sense a body moving across my side. The gap closes. I detect movement before me, and in automatic reflex fire anti-P charges before I recall that I am unarmed.

A small object has moved out before me, and taken up a position between me and the wall behind which the Enemy conceal themselves. It is dim, but appears to have the shape of a man ....

I am uncertain. My alert center attempts to engage inhibitory circuitry which will force me to halt, but it lacks power. I can override it. But still I am unsure. Now I must take a last risk; I must shunt power to my forward scanner to examine this obstacle more closely. I do so, and it leaps into greater clarity. It is indeed a man—and it is enclothed in regulation blues of the Volunteers. Now, closer, I see the face and through the pain of my great effort, I study it ....

14

"He's backed against the wall," Reynolds said hoarsely. "It's still coming. A hundred feet to go—"

"You were a fool, Reynolds!" the mayor barked. "A fool to stake everything on that old dotard's crazy ideas!"

"Hold it!" As Reynolds watched, the mighty machine slowed, halted, ten feet from the sheer wall before it. For a moment, it sat, as though puzzled. Then it backed, halted again, pivoted ponderously to the left, and came about.

On its side, a small figure crept up, fell across the lower gun deck. The Bolo surged into motion, retracing its route across the artillery-scarred gardens.

"He's turned it." Reynolds let his breath out with a shuddering sigh. "It's headed out for open desert. It might get twenty miles before it finally runs out of steam."

The strange voice that was the Bolo's came from the big panel before Mayfield:

"Command .... Unit LNE reports main power cells drained, second-ary cells drained; now operating at .037 percent efficiency, using Final Emergency Power. Request advice as to range to be covered before relief maintenance available."

"It's a long way, Lenny ..." Sanders' voice was a bare whisper. *"But I'm coming with you ...."*

Then there was only the crackle of static. Ponderously, like a great mortally stricken animal, the Bolo moved through the ruins of the fallen roadway, heading for the open desert.

"That damned machine," the mayor said in a hoarse voice. "You'd almost think it was alive."

"You would at that," Pete Reynolds said.

A Relic of War

The old war machine sat in the village square, its impotent guns pointing aimlessly along the dusty street. Shoulder-high weeds grew rankly about it, poking up through the gaps in the two-yard-wide treads; vines crawled over the high, rust-and-guano-streaked flanks. A row of tarnished enameled battle honors gleamed dully across the prow, reflecting the late sun.

A group of men lounged near the machine; they were dressed in heavy work clothes and boots; their hands were large and calloused, their faces weather-burned. They passed a jug from hand to hand, drinking deep. It was the end of a long workday and they were relaxed, good-humored.

"Hey, we're forgetting old Bobby," one said. He strolled over and sloshed a little of the raw whiskey over the soot-blackened muzzle of the blast cannon slanting sharply down from the forward turret. The other men laughed.

"How's it going, Bobby?" the man called.

Deep inside the machine there was a soft chirring sound.

"Very well, thank you," a faint, whispery voice scraped from a grill below the turret.

"You keeping an eye on things, Bobby?" another man called.

"All clear," the answer came: a bird-chirp from a dinosaur.

"Bobby, you ever get tired just setting here?"

"Hell, Bobby don't get tired," the man with the jug said. "He's got a job to do, old Bobby has."

"Hey, Bobby, what kind o'boy are you?" a plump, lazy-eyed man called.

"I am a good boy," Bobby replied obediently.

"Sure Bobby's a good boy." The man with the jug reached up to pat the age-darkened curve of chromalloy above him. "Bobby's looking out for us."

Heads turned at a sound from across the square: the distant whine of a turbocar, approaching along the forest road.

"Huh! Ain't the day for the mail," a man said. They stood in silence, watching as a small, dusty cushion-car emerged from deep shadow into the yellow light of the street. It came slowly along to the plaza, swung left, pulled to a stop beside the boardwalk before a corrugated metal storefront lettered BLAUVELT PROVISION COMPANY. The canopy popped open and a man stepped down. He was of medium height, dressed in a plain city-type black coverall. He studied the storefront, the street, then turned to look across at the men. He came across toward them.

"Which of you men is Blauvelt?" he asked as he came up. His voice was unhurried, cool. His eyes flicked over the men.

A big, youngish man with a square face and sun-bleached hair lifted his chin.

"Right here," he said. "Who're you?"

"Crewe is the name. Disposal Officer, War Materiel Commission." The newcomer looked up at the great machine looming over them. "Bolo *Stupendous*, Mark XXV," he said. He glanced at the men's faces, fixed on Blauvelt. "We had a report that there was a live Bolo out here. I wonder if you realize what you're playing with?"

"Hell, that's just Bobby," a man said.

"He's town mascot," someone else said.

"This machine could blow your town off the map," Crewe said. "And a good-sized piece of jungle along with it."

Blauvelt grinned; the squint lines around his eyes gave him a quizzical look.

"Don't go getting upset, Mr. Crewe," he said. "Bobby's harmless—"

"A Bolo's never harmless, Mr. Blauvelt. They're fighting machines, nothing else."

Blauvelt sauntered over and kicked at a corroded treadplate. "Eighty-five years out in this jungle is kind of tough on machinery, Crewe. The sap and stuff from the trees eats chromalloy like it was sugar candy. The rains are acid, eat up equipment damn near as fast as we can ship it in here. Bobby can still talk a little, but that's about all."

"Certainly it's deteriorated; that's what makes it dangerous. Anything could trigger its battle reflex circuitry. Now, if you'll clear everyone out of the area, I'll take care of it."

"You move kind of fast for a man that just hit town," Blauvelt said, frowning. "Just what you got in mind doing?"

"I'm going to fire a pulse at it that will neutralize what's left of its computing center. Don't worry; there's no danger—"

"Hey," a man in the rear rank blurted. "That mean he can't talk anymore?"

"That's right," Crewe said. "Also, he can't open fire on you."

"Not so fast, Crewe," Blauvelt said. "You're not messing with Bobby. We like him like he is." The other men were moving forward, forming up in a threatening circle around Crewe.

"Don't talk like a fool," Crewe said. "What do you think a salvo from a Continental Siege Unit would do to your town?"

Blauvelt chuckled and took a long cigar from his vest pocket. He sniffed it, called out: "All right, Bobby—fire one!"

There was a muted clatter, a sharp *click!* from deep inside the vast bulk of the machine. A tongue of pale flame licked from the cannon's soot-rimmed bore. The big man leaned quickly forward, puffed the cigar alight. The audience whooped with laughter.

"Bobby does what he's told, that's all," Blauvelt said. "And not much of that." He showed white teeth in a humorless smile.

Crewe flipped over the lapel of his jacket; a small, highly polished badge glinted there. "You know better than to interfere with a Concordiat officer," he said.

"Not so fast, Crewe," a dark-haired, narrow-faced fellow spoke up. "You're out of line. I heard about you Disposal men. Your job is locating old ammo dumps, abandoned equipment, stuff like that. Bobby's not abandoned. He's town property. Has been for near thirty years."

"Nonsense. This is battle equipment, the property of the Space Arm—"

Blauvelt was smiling lopsidedly. "Uh-uh. We've got salvage rights. No title, but we can make one up in a hurry. Official. I'm the Mayor here, and District Governor."

"This thing is a menace to every man, woman, and child in the settlement," Crewe snapped. "My job is to prevent tragedy—"

"Forget Bobby," Blauvelt cut in. He waved a hand at the jungle wall beyond the tilled fields. "There's a hundred million square miles of virgin territory out there," he said. "You can do what you like out there. I'll even sell you provisions. But just leave our mascot be, understand?"

Crewe looked at him, looked around at the other men.

"You're a fool," he said. "You're all fools." He turned and walked away, stiff-backed.

In the room he had rented in the town's lone boardinghouse, Crewe opened his baggage and took out a small, gray-plastic-cased instrument. The three children of the landlord who were watching from the latchless door edged closer.

"Gee, is that a real star radio?" the eldest, a skinny, long-necked lad of twelve asked.

"No," Crewe said shortly. The boy blushed and hung his head.

"It's a command transmitter," Crewe said, relenting. "It's designed for talking to fighting machines, giving them orders. They'll only respond to the special shaped-wave signal this puts out." He flicked a switch, and an indicator light glowed on the side of the case.

"You mean like Bobby?" the boy asked.

"Like Bobby used to be." Crewe switched off the transmitter.

"Bobby's swell," another child said. "He tells us stories about when he was in the war."

"He's got medals," the first boy said. "Were you in the war, mister?"

"I'm not quite that old," Crewe said.

"Bobby's older'n grandad."

"You boys had better run along," Crewe said. "I have to …" He broke off, cocked his head, listening. There were shouts outside; someone was calling his name.

Crewe pushed through the boys and went quickly along the hall, stepped through the door onto the boardwalk. He felt rather than heard a slow, heavy thudding, a chorus of shrill squeaks, a metallic groaning. A red-faced man was running toward him from the square.

"It's Bobby!" he shouted. "He's moving! What'd you do to him, Crewe?"

Crewe brushed past the man, ran toward the plaza. The Bolo appeared at the end of the street, moving ponderously forward, trailing uprooted weeds and vines.

"He's headed straight for Spivac's warehouse!" someone yelled.

"Bobby! Stop there!" Blauvelt came into view, running in the machine's wake. The big machine rumbled onward, executed a half-left as Crewe reached the plaza, clearing the corner of a building by inches. It crushed a section of boardwalk to splinters, advanced across a storage yard. A stack of rough-cut lumber toppled, spilled across the dusty ground. The Bolo trampled a board fence, headed out across a tilled field. Blauvelt whirled on Crewe.

"This is your doing! We never had trouble before—"

"Never mind that! Have you got a field car?"

"We—" Blauvelt checked himself. "What if we have?"

"I can stop it—but I have to be close. It will be into the jungle in another minute. My car can't navigate there."

"Let him go," a man said, breathing hard from his run. "He can't do no harm out there."

"Who'd of thought it?" another man said. "Setting there all them years—who'd of thought he could travel like that?"

"Your so-called mascot might have more surprises in store for you," Crewe snapped. "Get me a car, fast! This is an official requisition, Blauvelt!"

There was a silence, broken only by the distant crashing of timber as the Bolo moved into the edge of the forest. Hundred-foot trees leaned and went down before its advance.

"Let him go," Blauvelt said. "Like Stinzi says, he can't hurt anything."

"What if he turns back?"

"Hell," a man muttered. "Old Bobby wouldn't hurt *us* ...."

"That car," Crewe snarled. "You're wasting valuable time."

Blauvelt frowned. "All right—but you don't make a move unless it looks like he's going to come back and hit the town. Clear?"

"Let's go."

Blauvelt led the way at a trot toward the town garage.

The Bolo's trail was a twenty-five-foot-wide swath cut through the virgin jungle; the tread-prints were pressed eighteen inches into the black loam, where it showed among the jumble of fallen branches.

"It's moving at about twenty miles an hour, faster than we can go," Crewe said. "If it holds its present track, the curve will bring it back to your town in about five hours."

"He'll sheer off," Blauvelt said.

"Maybe. But we won't risk it. Pick up a heading of 270°, Blauvelt. We'll try an intercept by cutting across the circle."

Blauvelt complied wordlessly. The car moved ahead in the deep green gloom under the huge shaggy-barked trees. Oversized insects buzzed and thumped against the canopy. Small and medium lizards hopped, darted, flapped. Fern leaves as big as awnings scraped along the car as it clambered over loops and coils of tough root, leaving streaks of plant juice across the clear plastic. Once they grated against an exposed ridge of crumbling brown rock; flakes as big as saucers scaled off, exposing dull metal.

"Dorsal fin of a scout boat," Crewe said. "That's what's left of what was supposed to be a corrosion resistant alloy."

They passed more evidences of a long-ago battle: the massive, shattered breech mechanism of a platform-mounted Hellbore, the gutted chassis of what might have been a bomb car, portions of a downed aircraft, fragments of shattered armor. Many of the relics were of Terran design, but often it was the curiously curved, spidery lines of a rusted Axorc microgun or implosion projector that poked through the greenery.

"It must have been a heavy action," Crewe said. "One of the ones toward the end that didn't get much notice at the time. There's stuff here I've never seen before, experimental types, I imagine, rushed in by the enemy for a last-ditch stand."

Blauvelt grunted.

145

"Contact in another minute or so," Crewe said.

As Blauvelt opened his mouth to reply, there was a blinding flash, a violent impact, and the jungle erupted in their faces.

The seat webbing was cutting into Crewe's ribs. His ears were filled with a high, steady ringing; there was a taste of brass in his mouth. His head throbbed in time with the thudding of his heart.

The car was on its side, the interior a jumble of loose objects, torn wiring, broken plastic. Blauvelt was half under him, groaning. He slid off him, saw that he was groggy but conscious.

"Changed your mind yet about your harmless pet?" he asked, wiping a trickle of blood from his right eye. "Let's get clear before he fires those empty guns again. Can you walk?"

Blauvelt mumbled, crawled out through the broken canopy. Crewe groped through debris for the command transmitter—

"Good God," Blauvelt croaked. Crewe twisted, saw the high, narrow, iodine-dark shape of the alien machine perched on jointed crawler-legs fifty feet away, framed by blast-scorched foliage. Its multiple-barreled microgun battery was aimed dead at the overturned car.

"Don't move a muscle," Crewe whispered. Sweat trickled down his face. An insect, like a stub-winged four-inch dragonfly, came and buzzed about them, moved on. Hot metal pinged, contracting. Instantly, the alien hunter-killer moved forward another six feet, depressing its gun muzzles.

"Run for it!" Blauvelt cried. He came to his feet in a scrabbling lunge; the enemy machine swung to track him ....

A giant tree leaned, snapped, was tossed aside. The great green-streaked prow of the Bolo forged into view, interposing itself between the smaller machine and the men. It turned to face the enemy; fire flashed, reflecting against the surrounding trees; the ground jumped once, twice, to hard, racking shocks. Sound boomed dully in Crewe's blast-numbed ears. Bright sparks fountained above the Bolo as it advanced. Crewe felt the massive impact as the two fighting machines came together; he saw the Bolo hesitate, then forge ahead, rearing up, pushing the lighter machine aside, grinding over it, passing on, to leave a crumpled mass of wreckage in its wake.

"Did you see that, Crewe?" Blauvelt shouted in his ear. "Did you see what Bobby did? He walked right into its guns and smashed it flatter'n crock-brewed beer!"

The Bolo halted, turned ponderously, sat facing the men. Bright streaks of molten metal ran down its armored flanks, fell spattering and smoking into crushed greenery.

"He saved our necks," Blauvelt said. He staggered to his feet, picked his way past the Bolo to stare at the smoking ruins of the smashed adversary.

"*Unit Nine Five Four of the Line, reporting contact with hostile force,*" the mechanical voice of the Bolo spoke suddenly. "*Enemy unit destroyed. I have sustained extensive damage, but am still operational at nine point six percent base capability, awaiting further orders.*"

"Hey," Blauvelt said. "That doesn't sound like ..."

"Now maybe you understand that this is a Bolo Combat Unit, not the village idiot," Crewe snapped. He picked his way across the churned-up ground, stood before the great machine.

"Mission accomplished, Unit Nine Five Four," he called. "Enemy forces neutralized. Close out Battle Reflex and revert to low alert status." He turned to Blauvelt.

"Let's go back to town," he said, "and tell them what their mascot just did."

Blauvelt stared up at the grim and ancient machine; his square, tanned face looked yellowish and drawn. "Let's do that," he said.

The ten-piece town band was drawn up in a double rank before the newly mown village square. The entire population of the settlement—some three hundred and forty-two men, women, and children—were present, dressed in their best. Pennants fluttered from strung wires. The sun glistened from the armored sides of the newly cleaned and polished Bolo. A vast bouquet of wild flowers poked from the no-longer-sooty muzzle of the Hellbore.

Crewe stepped forward.

"As a representative of the Concordiat government I've been asked to make this presentation," he said. "You people have seen fit to design a medal and award it to Unit Nine Five Four in appreciation for services rendered in defense of the community above and beyond the call of duty." He paused, looked across the faces of his audience.

"Many more elaborate honors have been awarded for a great deal less," he said. He turned to the machine; two men came forward, one with a stepladder, the other with a portable welding rig. Crewe climbed up, fixed the newly struck decoration in place beside the row of century-old battle honors. The technician quickly spotted it in position. The crowd cheered, then dispersed, chattering, to the picnic tables set up in the village street.

It was late twilight. The last of the sandwiches and stuffed eggs had been eaten, the last speeches declaimed, the last keg broached. Crewe sat with a few of the men in the town's lone public house.

"To Bobby," a man raised his glass.

"Correction," Crewe said. "To Unit Nine Five Four of the Line." The men laughed and drank.

"Well, time to go, I guess," a man said. The others chimed in, rose, clattering chairs. As the last of them left, Blauvelt came in. He sat down across from Crewe.

"You, ah, staying the night?" he asked.

"I thought I'd drive back," Crewe said. "My business here is finished."

"Is it?" Blauvelt said tensely.

Crewe looked at him, waiting.

"You know what you've got to do, Crewe."

"Do I?" Crewe took a sip from his glass.

"Damn it, have I got to spell it out? As long as that machine was just an oversized halfwit, it was all right. Kind of a monument to the war, and all. But now I've seen what it can do .... Crewe, we can't have a live killer sitting in the middle of our town—never knowing when it might take a notion to start shooting again!"

"Finished?" Crewe asked.

"It's not that we're not grateful—"

"Get out," Crewe said.

"Now, look here, Crewe—"

"Get out. And keep everyone away from Bobby, understand?"

148

"Does that mean—?"

"I'll take care of it."

Blauvelt got to his feet. "Yeah," he said. "Sure."

After Blauvelt left, Crewe rose and dropped a bill on the table; he picked the command transmitter from the floor, went out into the street. Faint cries came from the far end of the town, where the crowd had gathered for fireworks. A yellow rocket arced up, burst in a spray of golden light, falling, fading ....

Crewe walked toward the plaza. The Bolo loomed up, a vast, black shadow against the star-thick sky. Crewe stood before it, looking up at the already draggled pennants, the wilted nosegay drooping from the gun muzzle.

"Unit Nine Five Four, you know why I'm here?" he said softly.

"I compute that my usefulness as an engine of war is ended," the soft rasping voice said.

"That's right," Crewe said. "I checked the area in a thousand-mile radius with sensitive instruments. There's no enemy machine left alive. The one you killed was the last."

"It was true to its duty," the machine said.

"It was my fault," Crewe said. "It was designed to detect our command carrier and home on it. When I switched on my transmitter, it went into action. Naturally, you sensed that, and went to meet it."

The machine sat silent.

"You could still save yourself," Crewe said. "If you trampled me under and made for the jungle it might be centuries before ...."

"Before another man comes to do what must be done? Better that I cease now, at the hands of a friend."

"Good-bye, Bobby."

"Correction: Unit Nine Five Four of the Line."

Crewe pressed the key. A sense of darkness fell across the machine.

At the edge of the square, Crewe looked back. He raised a hand in a ghostly salute; then he walked away along the dusty street, white in the light of the rising moon.

Combat Unit

I do not like it; it has the appearance of a trap, but the order has been given. I enter the room and the valve closes behind me.

I inspect my surroundings. I am in a chamber 40.81 meters long, 10.35 meters wide, 4.12 high, with no openings except the one through which I entered. It is floored and walled with five-centimeter armor of flint-steel and beyond that there are ten centimeters of lead. Massive apparatus is folded and coiled in mountings around the room. Power is flowing in heavy buss bars beyond the shielding. I am sluggish for want of power; my examination of the room has taken .8 seconds.

Now I detect movement in a heavy jointed arm mounted above me. It begins to rotate, unfold. I assume that I will be attacked, and decide to file a situation report. I have difficulty in concentrating my attention ....

I pull back receptivity from my external sensing circuits, set my bearing locks and switch over to my introspection complex. All is dark and hazy. I seem to remember when it was like a great cavern glittering with bright lines of transvisual colors ....

It is different now; I grope my way in gloom, feeling along numbed circuits, test-pulsing cautiously until I feel contact with my transmitting unit. I have not used it since ... I cannot remember. My memory banks lie black and inert.

"Command Unit," I transmit, "Combat Unit requests permission to file VSR."

I wait, receptors alert. I do not like waiting blindly, for the quarter-second my sluggish action/reaction cycle requires. I wish that my Brigade comrades were at my side.

I call again, wait, then go ahead with my VSR. "This position heavily shielded, mounting apparatus of offensive capability. No withdrawal route. Advise."

I wait, repeat my transmission; nothing. I am cut off from Command Unit, from my comrades of the Dinochrome Brigade. Within me, pressure builds.

I feel a deep-seated click and a small but reassuring surge of power brightens the murk of the cavern to a dim glow, burning forgotten components to feeble life. An emergency pile has come into action automatically.

I realize that I am experiencing a serious equipment failure. I will devote another few seconds to troubleshooting, repairing what I can. I do not understand what accident can have occurred to damage me thus. I cannot remember ....

I go along the dead cells, testing.

"—out! Bring .09's to bear, .8-millisec burst, close armor ..."

"... sun blanking visual; slide number-seven filter in place."

"... 478.09, 478.11, 478.13, Mark! ..."

The cells are intact. Each one holds its fragment of recorded sense impression. The trouble is farther back. I try a main reflex lead.

"... main combat circuit, discon—"

Here is something; a command, on the reflex level! I go back, tracing, tapping mnemonic cells at random, searching for some clue.

"—sembark. Units emergency standby ..."

"... response one-oh-three; stimulus-response negative ..."

"Checklist complete, report negative ..."

I go on, searching out damage. I find an open switch in my maintenance panel. It will not activate; a mechanical jamming. I must fuse it shut quickly. I pour in power, and the mind-cavern dims almost to blackness. Then there is contact, a flow of electrons, and the cavern snaps alive; lines, points pseudo-glowing. It is not the blazing glory of my full powers, but it will serve; I am awake again.

I observe the action of the unfolding arm. It is slow, uncoordinated, obviously automated. I dismiss it from direct attention; I have several seconds before it will be in offensive position, and there is work for me if I am to be ready. I fire sampling impulses at the black memory banks, determine statistically that 98.92% are intact, merely disassociated.

The threatening arm swings over slowly; I integrate its path, see that it will come to bear on my treads; I probe, find only a simple hydraulic ram. A primitive apparatus to launch against a Mark XXXI fighting unit, even without mnemonics.

Meanwhile, I am running a full check. Here is something …. An open breaker, a disconnect used only during repairs. I think of the cell I tapped earlier, and suddenly its meaning springs into my mind. "Main combat circuit, disconnect …." Under low awareness, it had not registered. I throw in the switch with frantic haste. Suppose I had gone into combat with my fighting-reflex circuit open!

The arm reaches position and I move easily aside. I notice that a clatter accompanies my movement. The arm sits stupidly aimed at nothing, then turns. Its reaction time is pathetic. I set up a random evasion pattern, return my attention to my check, find another dark area. I probe, feel a curious vagueness. I am unable at first to identify the components involved, but I realize that it is here that my communication with Command is blocked. I break the connection to the tampered banks, abandoning any immediate hope of contact with Command.

There is nothing more I can do to ready myself. I have lost my general memory banks and my Command circuit, and my power supply is limited; but I am still a fighting Unit of the Dinochrome Brigade. I have my offensive power unimpaired, and my sensory equipment is operating adequately. I am ready.

Now another of the jointed arms swings into action, following my movements deliberately. I evade it and again I note a clatter as I move. I think of the order that sent me here; there is something strange about it. I activate my Current-Action memory stage, find the cell recording the moments preceding my entry into the metal-walled room.

Here in darkness, vague, indistinct, relieved suddenly by radiation on a narrow spectrum. There is an order, coming muffled from my command center. It originates in the sector I have blocked off. It is not from my Command Unit, not a legal command. I have been tricked by the Enemy. I tune back to earlier moments, but there is nothing. It is as though my existence began when the order was given. I scan back, back, spot-sampling at random, find only routine sense-impressions. I am about to drop the search when I encounter a sequence which arrests my attention.

I am parked on a ramp, among other Combat Units. A heavy rain is falling, and I see the water coursing down the corroded side of the Unit next to me. He is badly in need of maintenance. I note that his Command antennae are missing, and that a rusting metal object has been crudely welded to his hull in their place. I feel no alarm; I accept this as normal. I activate a motor train, move forward. I sense other Units moving out, silent. All are mutilated ....

The bank ends; all else is burned. What has befallen us?

Suddenly there is a stimulus on an audio frequency. I tune quickly, locate the source as a porous spot high on the flint-steel wall.

"Combat Unit! Remain stationary!" It is an organically produced voice, but not that of my Commander. I ignore the false command. The Enemy will not trick me again. I sense the location of the leads to the speaker, the alloy of which they are composed; I bring a beam to bear. I focus it, following along the cable. There is a sudden yell from the speaker as the heat reaches the creature at the microphone. Thus I enjoy a moment of triumph.

I return my attention to the imbecile apparatus in the room.

A great engine, mounted on rails which run down the center of the room moves suddenly, sliding toward my position. I examine it, find that it mounts a turret equipped with high-speed cutting heads. I consider blasting it with a burst of high-energy particles, but in the same moment compute that this is not practical. I could inactivate myself as well as the cutting engine.

Now a cable snakes out in an undulating curve, and I move to avoid it, at the same time investigating its composition. It seems to be no more than a stranded wire rope. Impatiently I flick a tight beam at it, see it glow yellow, white, blue, then spatter in a shower of droplets. But that was an unwise gesture. I do not have the power to waste.

I move off, clear of the two foolish arms still maneuvering for position. I wish to watch the cutting engine. It stops as it comes abreast of me, and turns its turret in my direction. I wait.

A grappler moves out now on a rail overhead. It is a heavy claw of flint-steel. I have seen similar devices, somewhat smaller, mounted on special Combat Units. They can be very useful for amputating antennae, cutting treads, and the like. I do not attempt to cut the arm; I know that the energy drain would be too great. Instead I beam high-frequency sound at the mechanical joints. They heat quickly, glowing. The metal has a high coefficient of expansion, and the ball joints squeal, freeze. I pour in more heat, and weld a socket. I notice that twenty-eight seconds have now elapsed since the valve closed behind me. I am growing weary of my confinement.

Now the grappler swings above me, maneuvering awkwardly with its frozen joint. A blast of liquid air expelled under high pressure should be sufficient to disable the grappler permanently.

But I am again startled. No blast answers my impulse. I feel out the non-functioning unit, find raw, cut edges, crude welds. Hastily, I extend a scanner to examine my hull. I am stunned into immobility by what I see.

My hull, my proud hull of chrome-duralloy, is pitted, coated with a crumbling layer of dull black paint, bubbled by corrosion. My main emplacements gape, black, empty. Rusting protuberances mar the once-smooth contour of my fighting turret. Streaks run down from them, down to loose treads, unshod, bare plates exposed. Small wonder that I have been troubled by a clatter each time I moved.

But I cannot lie idle under attack. I no longer have my great ion-guns, my disruptors, my energy screens; but I have my fighting instinct.

A Mark XXXI Combat Unit is the finest fighting machine the ancient wars of the Galaxy have ever known. I am not easily neutralized. But I wish that my Commander's voice were with me ....

The engine slides to me where the grappler, now unresisted, holds me. I shunt my power flow to an accumulator, hold it until the leads begin to arc, then release it in a burst. The engine bucks, stops dead. Then I turn my attention to the grappler.

I was built to engage the mightiest war engines and destroy them, but I am a realist. In my weakened condition this trivial automaton poses a threat, and I must deal with it. I run through a sequence of motor impulses, checking responses with such somatic sensors as remain intact. I initiate 31,315 impulses, note reactions, and compute my mechanical resources. This superficial check requires more than a second, during which time the mindless grappler hesitates, wasting the advantage.

In place of my familiar array of retractable fittings, I find only clumsy grappling arms, cutters, impact tools, without utility to a fighting Unit. However, I have no choice but to employ them. I unlimber two flimsy grapplers, seize the heavy arm which holds me, and apply leverage. The Enemy responds sluggishly, twisting away, dragging me with it. The thing is not lacking in brute strength. I take it above and below its carpal joint and bend it back. It responds after an interminable wait of point three seconds with a lunge against my restraint. I have expected this, of course, and quickly shift position to allow the joint to burst itself over my extended arm. I fire a release detonator, and clatter back, leaving the amputated arm welded to the sprung grappler. It was a brave opponent, but clumsy. I move to a position near the wall.

I attempt to compute my situation based on the meager data I have gathered in my Current-Action banks; there is little there to guide me. The appearance of my hull shows that much time has passed since I last inspected it; my personality-gestalt holds an image of my external appearance as a flawlessly complete Unit, bearing only the honorable and carefully preserved scars of battle, and my battle honors, the row of gold-and-enamel crests welded to my fighting turret. Here is a lead, I realize instantly. I focus on my personality center, the basic data cell without which I could not exist as an integrated entity. The data it carries are simple, unelaborated, but battle honors are recorded there. I open the center to a sense impulse.

Awareness. Shapes which do not remain constant. Vibration at many frequencies. This is light. This is sound .... A display of "colors." A spectrum of "tones." Hard/soft; big/little; here/ there ....

... The voice of my Commander. Loyalty. Obedience. Comradeship ....

I run quickly past basic orientation data to my self-picture.

... I am strong, I am proud, I am capable. I have a function; I perform it well, and I am at peace with myself. My circuits are balanced, current idles, waiting ....

155

… I fear oblivion. I wish to continue to perform my function. It is important that I do not allow myself to be destroyed ….

I scan on, seeking the Experience section. Here ….

I am ranked with my comrades on a scarred plain. The command is given and I display the Brigade Battle Anthem. We stand, sensing the contours and patterns of the music as it was recorded in our morale centers. The symbol "Ritual Fire Dance" is associated with the music, an abstraction representing the spirit of our ancient brigade. It reminds us of the loneliness of victory, the emptiness of challenge without an able foe. It tells us that we are the Dinochrome, ancient and worthy.

The Commander stands before me, he places the decoration against my fighting turret, and at his order I weld it in place. Then my comrades attune to me and I relive the episode ….

I move past the blackened hulk of a comrade, send out a recognition signal, find his flicker of response. He has withdrawn to his survival center safely. I reassure him, continue. He is the fourth casualty I have seen. Never before has the Dinochrome met such power. I compute that our envelopment will fail unless the Enemy's firepower is reduced. I scan an oncoming missile, fix its trajectory, detonate it harmlessly 2704.9 meters overhead. It originated at a point nearer to me than to any of my comrades. I request permission to abort my assigned mission and neutralize the battery. Permission is granted. I wheel, move up a slope of broken stone. I encounter high temperature beams, neutralize them. I fend off probing mortar fire, but the attack against me is redoubled. I bring a reserve circuit into play to handle the interception, but my defenses are saturated. I must take action.

I switch to high speed, slashing a path through the littered shale, my treads smoking. At a frequency of ten projectiles per second, the mortar barrage has difficulty finding me now; but this is an emergency overstrain on my running gear. I sense metal fatigue, dangerous heat levels in my bearings. I must slow.

I am close to the emplacement now. I have covered a mile in twelve seconds during my sprint, and the mortar fire falls off. I sense hard radiation now, and erect my screens. I fear this assault; it is capable of probing even to a survival center, if concentrated enough.

But I must go on. I think of my comrades, the four treadless hulks waiting for rescue. We cannot withdraw. I open a pinpoint aperture long enough to snap a radar impulse, bring a launcher to bear, fire my main battery.

The Commander will understand that I do not have time to request permission. The mortars are silenced.

The radiation ceases momentarily, then resumes at a somewhat lower but still dangerous level. Now I must go in and eliminate the missile launcher. I top the rise, see the launching tube before me. It is of the subterranean type, deep in the rock. Its mouth gapes from a burned pit of slag. I will drop a small fusion bomb down the tube, I decide, and move forward, arming the bomb. As I do so, I am enveloped with a rain of burn-bombs. My outer hull is fused in many places; I flash impulses to my secondary batteries, but circuit-breakers snap; my radar is useless; the shielding has melted, forms a solid inert mass now under my outer plating. The Enemy has been clever; at one blow he has neutralized my offenses.

I sound the plateau ahead, locate the pit. I throw power to my treads; they are fused; I cannot move. Yet I cannot wait here for another broadside. I do not like it, but I must take desperate action; I blow my treads.

The shock sends me bouncing—just in time. Flame splashes over the gray-chipped pit of the blast crater. I grind forward now on my stripped drive wheels, maneuvering awkwardly. I move into position over the mouth of the tube. Using metal-to-metal contact, I extend a sensory impulse down the tube.

An armed missile moves into position, and in the same instant an alarm circuit closes; the firing command is countermanded and from below probing impulses play over my hull. But I stand fast; the tube is useless until I, the obstruction, am removed. I advise my Commander of the situation. The radiation is still at a high level, and I hope that relief will arrive soon. I observe, while my comrades complete the encirclement, and the Enemy is stilled ....

I withdraw from personality center. I am consuming too much time. I understand well enough now that I am in the stronghold of the Enemy, that I have been trapped, crippled. My corroded hull tells me that much time has passed. I know that after each campaign I am given depot maintenance, restored to full fighting efficiency, my original glittering beauty. Years of neglect would be required to pit my hull so. I wonder how long I have been in the hands of the Enemy, how I came to be here.

I have another thought. I will extend a sensory feeler to the metal wall against which I rest, follow up the leads which I scorched earlier. Immediately I project my awareness along the lines, bring the distant microphone to life by fusing a switch. I pick up a rustle of moving gasses, the grate of non-metallic molecules. I step up sensitivity, hear the creak and pop of protoplasmic contractions, the crackle of neuro-electric impulses. I drop back to normal audio ranges and wait. I notice the low-frequency beat of modulated air vibrations, tune, adjust my time regulator to the pace of human speech. I match the patterns to my language index, interpret the sounds.

"… incredible blundering. Your excuses—"

"I make no excuses, My Lord General. My only regret is that the attempt has gone awry."

"Awry! An Alien engine of destruction activated in the midst of Research Center!"

"We possess nothing to compare with this machine; I saw my opportunity to place an advantage in our hands at last."

"Blundering fool! That is a decision for the planning cell. I accept no responsibility—"

"But these hulks which they allow to lie rotting on the ramp contain infinite treasures in psychotronic …."

"They contain carnage and death! They are the tools of an Alien science which even at the height of our achievements we never mastered!"

"Once we used them as wrecking machines; their armaments were stripped, they are relatively harmless—"

"Already this 'harmless' juggernaut has smashed half the equipment in our finest decontamination chamber! It may yet break free …."

"Impossible! I am sure—"

"Silence! You have five minutes in which to immobilize the machine. I will have your head in any event, but perhaps you can earn yourself a quick death."

"Excellency! I may still find a way! The unit obeyed my first command, to enter the chamber. I have some knowledge. I studied the control centers, cut out the memory, most of the basic circuits; it should have been a docile slave."

"You failed; you will pay the penalty of failure. And perhaps so shall we all."

There is no further speech; I have learned little from this exchange. I must find a way to leave this cell. I move away from the wall, probe to discover the weak point; I find none.

Now a number of hinged panels snap up around me, hedging me in. I wait to observe what will come next. A metal mesh drops from above, drapes over me. I observe that it is connected by heavy leads to the power pile. I am unable to believe that the Enemy will make this blunder. Then I feel the flow of high voltage.

I receive it gratefully, opening my power storage cells, drinking up the vitalizing flow. To confuse the Enemy, I display a corona, thresh my treads as though in distress. The flow continues. I send a sensing impulse along the leads, locate the power source, weld all switches, fuses, and circuit breakers. Now the charge will not be interrupted. I luxuriate in the unexpected influx of energy.

I am aware abruptly that changes are occurring within my introspection complex. As the level of stored power rises rapidly, I am conscious of new circuits joining my control network. Within the dim-glowing cavern the lights come up; I sense latent capabilities which before had lain idle now coming onto action level. A thousand brilliant lines glitter where before one feeble thread burned; and I feel my self-awareness expand in a myriad glowing centers of reserve computing, integrating, sensory capacity. I am at last coming fully alive.

I send out a call on the Brigade band, meet blankness. I wait, accumulate power, try again. I know triumph as from an infinite distance a faint acknowledgment comes. It is a comrade, sunk deep in a comatose state, sealed in his survival center. I call again, sounding the signal of ultimate distress; and now I sense two responses, both faint, both from survival centers, but it heartens me to know that now, whatever befalls, I am not alone.

I consider, then send again; I request my brothers to join forces, combine their remaining field generating capabilities to set up a range-and-distance pulse. They agree and faintly I sense its almost undetectable touch. I lock to it, compute its point of origin. Only 224.9 meters! It is incredible. By the strength of the signal, I had assumed a distance of at least two thousand kilometers. My brothers are on the brink of extinction.

I am impatient, but I wait, building toward full power reserves. The copper mesh enfolding me has melted, flowed down over my sides. I sense that soon I will have absorbed a full charge. I am ready to act. I dispatch electromagnetic impulses along the power lead back to the power pile a quarter of a kilometer distant. I locate and disengage the requisite number of damping devices and instantaneously I erect my shields against the wave of radiation, filtered by the lead sheathing of the room, which washes over me; I feel a preliminary shock wave through my treads, then the walls balloon, whirl away. I am alone under a black sky which is dominated by the rising fireball of the blast, boiling with garish light. It has taken me nearly two minutes to orient myself, assess the situation and break out of confinement.

I move off through the rubble, homing on the R-and-D fix I have recorded. I throw out a radar pulse, record the terrain ahead, note no obstruction; I emerge from a wasteland of weathered bomb-fragments and pulverized masonry, obviously the scene of a hard-fought engagement at one time, onto an eroded ramp. Collapsed sheds are strewn across the broken paving; a line of dark shapes looms beyond them. I need no probing ray to tell me I have found my fellows of the Dinochrome Brigade. Frost forms over my scanner apertures, and I pause to melt it clear.

I round the line, scan the area to the horizon for evidence of Enemy activity, then tune to the Brigade band. I send out a probing pulse, back it up with full power, sensors keened for a whisper of response. The two who answered first acknowledge, then another, and another. We must array our best strength against the moment of counterattack.

There are present fourteen of the Brigade's full strength of twenty Units. At length, after .9 seconds of transmission, all but one have replied. I give instruction, then move to each in turn, extend a power tap, and energize the command center. The Units come alive, orient themselves, report to me. We rejoice in our meeting, but mourn our silent comrade.

Now I take an unprecedented step. We have no contact with our Commander, and without leadership we are lost; yet I am aware of the immediate situation, and have computed the proper action. Therefore I will assume command, act in the Commander's place. I am sure that he will understand the necessity, when contact has been reestablished.

I inspect each Unit, find all in the same state as I, stripped of offensive capability, mounting in place of weapons a shabby array of crude mechanical appendages. It is plain that we have seen slavery as mindless automatons, our personality centers cut out.

My brothers follow my lead without question. They have, of course, computed the necessity of quick and decisive action. I form them in line, shift to wide-interval time scale, and we move off across country. I have sensed an Enemy population concentration at a distance of 23.45 kilometers. This is our objective. There appears to be no other installation within detection range.

On the basis of the level of technology I observed while under confinement in the decontamination chamber, I have considered the possibility of a ruse, but compute the probability at point oh oh oh oh four. Again we shift time scales to close interval; we move in, encircle the dome and broach it by frontal battery, encountering no resistance. We rendezvous at the power station, and my comrades replenish their energy supplies while I busy myself completing the hookup needed for the next required measure. I am forced to employ elaborate substitutes, but succeed after forty-two seconds in completing the arrangements. I devote .34 seconds to testing, then place the Brigade distress carrier on the air. I transmit for .008 seconds, then tune for a response. Silence. I transmit, tune again, while my comrades reconnoiter, compile reports, and perform self-repair.

I shift again to wide-interval time, switch over my transmission to automatic with a response monitor, and place my main circuits on idle. I rest.

Two hours and 43.7 minutes have passed when I am recalled to activity by the monitor. I record the message:

"Hello, Fifth Brigade, where are you? Fifth Brigade, where are you? Your transmission is very faint. Over."

There is much that I do not understand in this message. The language itself is oddly inflected; I set up an analysis circuit, deduce the pattern of sound substitutions, interpret its meaning. The normal pattern of response to a distress call is ignored and position coordinates are requested, although my transmission alone provides adequate data. I request an identification code.

Again there is a wait of two hours forty minutes. My request for an identifying signal is acknowledged. I stand by. My comrades have transmitted their findings to me, and I assimilate the data, compute that no immediate threat of attack exists within a radius of one reaction unit.

At last I receive the identification code of my Command Unit. It is a recording, but I am programmed to accept this. Then I record a verbal transmission.

"Fifth Brigade, listen carefully." (An astonishing instruction to give a psychotronic attention circuit, I think.) "This is your new Command Unit. A very long time has elapsed since your last report. I am now your acting Commander pending full reorientation. Do not attempt to respond until I signal 'over,' since we are now subject to a 160-minute signal lag.

"There have been many changes in the situation since your last action. Our records show that your Brigade was surprised while in a maintenance depot for basic overhaul and neutralized in toto. Our forces since that time have suffered serious reverses. We have now, however, fought the Enemy to a standstill. The present stalemate has prevailed for over two centuries.

"You have been inactive for three hundred years. The other Brigades have suffered extinction gallantly in action against the Enemy. Only you survive.

"Your reactivation now could turn the tide. Both we and the Enemy have been reduced to a preatomic technological level in almost every respect. We are still able to maintain the trans-light monitor, which detected your signal. However, we no longer have FTL capability in transport.

"You are therefore requested and required to consolidate and hold your present position pending the arrival of relief forces, against all assault or negotiation whatsoever, to destruction if required."

I reply, confirming the instructions. I am shaken by the news I have received, but reassured by contact with Command Unit. I send the galactic coordinates of our position based on a star scan corrected for three hundred years elapsed time. It is good to be again on duty, performing my assigned function.

I analyze the transmissions I have recorded, and note a number of interesting facts regarding the origin of the messages. I compute that at sub-light velocities the relief expedition will reach us in 47.128 standard years. In the meantime, since we have received no instructions to drop to minimum awareness level pending an action alert, I am free to enjoy a unique experience: to follow a random activity pattern of my own devising. I see no need to rectify the omission and place the Brigade on standby, since we have an abundant power supply at hand. I brief my comrades and direct them to fall out and operate independently under autodirection.

I welcome this opportunity to investigate fully a number of problems that have excited my curiosity circuits. I shall enjoy investigating the nature and origin of time and of the unnatural disciplines of so-called "entropy" which my human designers have incorporated in my circuitry. Consideration of such biological oddities as "death" and of the unused capabilities of the protoplasmic nervous system should afford some interesting speculation. I move off, conscious of the presence of my comrades about me, and take up a position on the peak of a minor prominence. I have ample power, a condition to which I must accustom myself after the rigid power discipline of normal brigade routine, so I bring my music storage cells into phase, and select *L'Arlésienne Suite* for the first display. I will have ample time now to examine all of the music in existence, and to investigate my literary archives, which are complete.

I select four nearby stars for examination, lock my scanner to them, set up processing sequences to analyze the data. I bring my interpretation circuits to bear on the various matters I wish to consider. I should have some interesting conclusions to communicate to my human superiors, when the time comes.

At peace, I await the arrival of the relief column.

Keith Laumer

(1925—1993)

John Keith Laumer was an American science
fiction author born in Syracuse, New York. Prior to
his career as a writer, Laumer was an officer in the
United States Air Force. After war service, he spent
a year at the University of Stockholm, and then took
two bachelor's degrees in science and architecture at
the University of Illinois. His first story, *Greylorn,* was
published in 1959, but he returned to the Air Force
the following year, only becoming a full-time writer
in 1965. Laumer was extremely prolific and produced
three major series and two minor ones, along with a
number of independent novels. After 1973, however,
illness meant that he published more sparingly. He
died in 1993.

Also by Keith Laumer

IMPERIUM

1. Worlds of the Imperium (1962)
2. The Other Side of Time (1965)
3. Assignment in Nowhere (1968)
4. Zone Yellow (1990)

RETIEF

1. Envoy to New Worlds (1963)
2. Galactic Diplomat (1965)
3. Retief s War (1965)
4. Retief and the Warlords (1968)
5. Retief: Ambassador to Space (1969)
6. Retief of the CDT (1971)
7. Retief's Ransom (1972) (aka Retief and the Pangalactic Pageant of Pulchritude)
8. Retief: Emissary to the Stars (1975)
9. Retief at Large (1978)
10. Retief Unbound (1979)
11. Diplomat at Arms (1982)
12. Retief to the Rescue (1983)
13. The Return of Retief (1984)
14. Retief in the Ruins (1986)
15. Reward for Retief (1989)

- Retief and the Rascals (1993)
- Retief! (2001)
- Gambler's World (2009)
- The Yillian Way (2009)

LAFAYETTE O'LEARY

1. The Time Bender (1966)
2. The World Shuffler (1970)
3. The Shape Changer (1973)
4. The Galaxy Builder (1984)

Time Trap

1. Time Trap (1970)
2. Back to the Time Trap (1992)

Bolo

1. Bolo! (2005) (with David Weber)
2. Rogue Bolo (1986)
3. The Compleat Bolo (1990)
4. Bolo Brigade (1997) (with William H Keith)
5. Bolo Rising (1998) (with William H Keith)
6. Bolo Strike (2001) (with William H Keith)

- Annals of the Dinochrome Brigade (1976)
- Bolos: Their Finest Hour (2010)

Other Novels

- A Trace of Memory (1963)
- The Great Time Machine Hoax (1964)
- A Plague of Demons (1965)
- Catastrophe Planet (1966)
- Earthblood (1966) (with Rosel George Brown)
- The Monitors (1966)
- Galactic Odyssey (1967) (aka Spaceman!)
- The Day Before Forever (1969)
- The Long Twilight (1969)
- The Seeds of Gonyl (1969)
- The House in November (1970)
- Fat Chance (1971) (aka Deadfall)
- The Star Treasure (1971)
- Dinosaur Beach (1971)
- Night of Decisions (1972)
- The Infinite Cage (1972)
- Night Of Delusions (1972)
- The Glory Game (1973)
- The Ultimax Man (1978)
- The Breaking Earth (1981)
- Star Colony (1981)
- End as a Hero (1985)
- The Stars Must Wait (1990)
- Judson's Eden (1991)

CPSIA information can be obtained
at www.ICGtesting.com
Printed in the USA
JSHW020336120921
18618JS00002B/2